Jonas would make
she'd done.

He'd make sure Ravenna learned the value of the money she'd taken, and when he'd finished with her she'd understand the value of hard work, too. She'd repay her debt in full. There'd be no easy escape if she tried batting those long eyelashes at him.

The realization stilled his impetuous need to taste her. Yet he couldn't draw back. He was trapped by a hunger sharper and more potent than he'd known in years.

That infuriated him even more than the missing money. He burned with it, the fire in his belly white-hot with a virulent mix of lust and self-disgust at his weakness.

At His Service

From glass slippers to silk sheets

From washing his sheets to slipping between them, from ironing his shirts to ripping them off.... When the job description said full benefits package, this wasn't quite what she had in mind!

But when you work for a man who's used to getting everything he wants, how do you stop yourself becoming his latest acquisition?

In May you read:

Maid for Montero by Kim Lawrence

This month read:

An Enticing Debt to Pay by Annie West

Look out for more At His Service stories, coming soon!

Annie West

—

An Enticing Debt to Pay

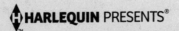

Recycling programs
for this product may
not exist in your area.

ISBN-13: 978-0-373-13187-7

AN ENTICING DEBT TO PAY

Copyright © 2013 by Annie West

Printed in U.S.A.

All about the author...
Annie West

ANNIE WEST spent her childhood with her nose between the covers of a book—a habit she retains. After years spent preparing government reports and official correspondence, she decided to write something she *really* enjoys. And there's nothing she loves more than a great romance. Despite her office-bound past she has managed a few interesting moments—including a marriage offer with the promise of a herd of camels to sweeten the contract. She is happily married to her ever-patient husband (who has never owned a dromedary). They live with their two children among the tall eucalypts at beautiful Lake Macquarie, on Australia's east coast. You can contact Annie through her website, www.annie-west.com, or write to her at P.O. Box 1041, Warners Bay, NSW 2282, Australia.

Other titles by Annie West available in ebook format:

CAPTIVE IN THE SPOTLIGHT
IMPRISONED BY A VOW
GIRL IN THE BEDOUIN TENT *(Sinful Desert Nights)*
UNDONE BY HIS TOUCH *(Dark-Hearted Tycoons)*

For dearest Claire

whose hard work, exuberance and sheer talent
are an inspiration.

With love.

CHAPTER ONE

'I'M AFRAID THE latest audit has thrown up an…irregularity.'

Jonas looked across his wide, polished desk and frowned as his Head of Finance shifted uncomfortably in his seat.

What sort of *irregularity* could make Charles Barker palpably nervous? He was the best. Jonas made it a policy only to employ the best. He didn't have patience for underperformers. Barker ran his part of Jonas' business enterprise like a well-oiled machine.

'A significant irregularity?'

Barker shook his head. 'Not in overall financial terms.'

Since the company's total assets figured in the billions, Jonas supposed he should be relieved, but watching Barker loosen his tie, Jonas felt a prickle of foreboding.

'Spit it out, Charles.'

The other man smiled, but it turned into a grimace as he passed his laptop across the desk.

'There. The top two lines.'

Jonas noted the first entry—a transfer of several thousand pounds. Below it another, much larger entry. No details were provided for either.

'What am I looking at?'

'Withdrawals against your original investment account.'

Jonas' frown became a scowl. He used that account now only to transfer personal funds between investments.

'Someone accessed my account?' But the answer was ob-

vious. Jonas hadn't made these withdrawals. He managed
day-to-day expenses elsewhere and, though large by normal standards, the withdrawals weren't significant enough
to match his usual personal investments.

'We've traced them.' Of course, Barker would make it
his business to have an answer before he fronted Jonas with
the problem.

'And?' Curiosity rose.

'You'll remember the account was originally set up as
part of a family enterprise.'

How could Jonas forget? His father had given him chapter
and verse on how to run a business, pretending he, as head
of the family, was the senior partner in the enterprise. But
they'd both known it was Jonas' talent for spotting a sound
investment, and his ruthless hunger for success, that had
turned the floundering investment company around. Piers
had simply been along for the ride, revelling in the novelty
of success. Until father and son had parted ways.

'I remember.' Memory was a sour tang on his tongue.

Barker shifted again. 'The withdrawals were made
using an old cheque book—one that had supposedly been
destroyed.' Jonas looked up, catching a faint flush on the
other man's cheeks. 'The records show they were accounted
for but this one of your father's…'

'It's okay, I get the picture.' Jonas let his gaze drift across
the unrivalled view of the City of London.

His father. Jonas hadn't called him that since childhood
when he'd discovered what sort of man Piers Deveson was.
Despite his bluster about honour and the family name, Piers
had been no model of virtue. It shouldn't surprise Jonas to
learn the old man had found a way to access his son's assets
illegally. The wonder was he hadn't used it earlier.

'So Piers—'

'No!' Barker sat straighter as Jonas turned back to him.
'I'm sorry, but we've reason to believe it wasn't your father.
Here.' He passed some photocopied pages across.

Jonas scanned them. Two cheques with his father's familiar flourishing signature.

Except they *weren't* Piers Deveson's signature. They were close enough to fool a stranger but he was familiar enough with that scrawl to spot the differences.

'Look at the dates.'

Jonas did and to his surprise felt a punch to the gut that winded him.

Bad enough to think the old man had pilfered funds. But this was—

Jonas shook his head, his lungs cramping as unexpected emotion filled him.

'The second one is dated a day after your father died.'

Silently Jonas nodded, his heart slowing to a ponderous beat. He knew the date, and not just because it was recent.

For years his father had been a thorn in his side, a blot on the family—living in gaudy luxury with his scheming mistress. They'd flaunted themselves among the rich and notorious, uncaring of any hurt they'd caused. When Piers died Jonas had felt nothing—neither regret nor an easing of the tension that had gripped him since Piers' defection had taken its ultimate toll. He'd expected to feel *something*. For weeks there'd been nothing, just an emptiness where emotion should have been. Yet now—

'Not my father then.' His voice was calm, belying the raw emotions churning in his gut. Beneath the desk his hands clenched.

'No. We've traced the perpetrator. And she's not too clever, given the obvious anomaly with the date.' Barker spoke quickly, obviously eager to get this over. 'It was a Ms Ruggiero. Living at this address in Paris.'

Barker handed over another paper. It bore the address of the exclusive apartment Piers Deveson had shared for the last six years with his mistress, Silvia Ruggiero.

Jonas paused before reaching out to take the paper. His fingers tingled as if it burned him.

'So.' Jonas sat back. 'My father's whore thinks she can continue to milk his family even after his death.' His voice was devoid of emotion, but he felt it deep inside like the burn of ice on bruised flesh.

How could the woman think she'd get away with this after all she'd done to the Devesons? Surely she wasn't stupid enough to expect mercy?

His pulse thudded as he thought of the woman who'd destroyed so much.

He remembered Silvia Ruggiero as clearly as if he'd seen her yesterday, her voluptuous figure, flashing eyes and froth of dark hair. Sex on legs, one of his friends had said the first time he'd seen Silvia, who was then the Devesons' housekeeper. And he'd been right. Not even a drab uniform had doused the woman's vibrant sexuality.

That had been mere weeks before Jonas' father had turned his back on family and responsibility, let alone respectability, by running off with his housekeeper to set her up in a luxury Paris apartment.

Four months later Jonas' mother was found dead. An accidental overdose, the coroner had said. But Jonas knew the truth. After years spurned by the man she'd loved, his public repudiation had finally been too much. His mother had taken her own life.

Jonas breathed deep, pulling oxygen into cramped lungs. Now the woman responsible for his mother's death had struck again. She had the nerve to think she could continue to steal from him!

The paper in his hand crackled as his fist tightened slowly, inexorably. Fury surged, tensing every sinew. His jaw ached as he clenched his teeth against a rising tide of useless invective.

Jonas never wasted energy on words when actions were so much more effective.

For six years he'd spurned the idea of revenge. He'd risen

above that temptation, burying himself in work and refusing any contact with Piers or his gold-digging mistress.

But now this—the straw that broke the camel's back.

The blood raced hot and sharp in his veins as for the first time Jonas allowed himself to contemplate fully the pleasures of retribution.

'Leave this to me, Charles.' Jonas smiled slowly, his facial muscles pulling tight. 'There's no need to report the fraud. I'll sort it out personally.'

Ravenna surveyed the apartment in despair. Most of the furnishings she knew now were fake, from the gilded Louis Quinze chairs to the china masquerading as period Limoges and Sèvres.

Mamma had always been adept at making ends meet, even through the toughest times.

A reluctant smile tugged Ravenna's lips. Life in a swanky apartment in the Place des Vosges, one of Paris's premier addresses, hardly counted as tough, not like the early days of Ravenna's childhood when food had been scarce and the winters cold without enough blankets or warm clothes. But those early experiences had stood her mother in good stead. When the money began to run out she'd methodically turned to replacing the priceless antiques with copies.

Silvia Ruggiero had always made do, even if her version of 'making do' lately had been on a preposterously luxurious scale. But it was what Piers had wanted and in Silvia's eyes that was all that mattered.

Ravenna tugged in a shaky breath. Her mother was far better off in Italy staying with a friend, instead of here, coping with the aftermath of Piers' death. If only she'd told Ravenna straight away about his heart attack. Ravenna would have been here the same day. Even now she could barely believe her mother had kept that to herself, worrying instead about disturbing Ravenna with more trouble!

Mothers! Did they ever believe their children grew up?

Silvia had been barely recognisable when Ravenna had arrived in Paris from Switzerland. For the first time her gorgeous mother had looked older than her age, worn by grief. Ravenna was concerned for her. Piers might not have been Ravenna's favourite but her mother had loved him.

No, Mamma was better off out of this. Packing up here was the least Ravenna could do, especially after Piers' generosity when she most needed it. So what if it meant facing creditors and selling what little her mother had left?

She returned to her inventory, glad she'd organised for an expert to visit and separate any valuable items from the fakes. To Ravenna they all looked obscenely expensive and rather ostentatious. But since her home was a sparsely furnished bedsit in a nondescript London suburb, she was no judge.

Jonas pressed the security buzzer a second time, wondering if she was out and his spur of the moment trip to Paris had been an impetuous waste of time.

He didn't do impetuous. He was methodical, measured and logical. But he also had a razor-sharp instinct for weakness, for the optimum time to strike. And surely now, mere weeks after Piers' death, his father's mistress would be feeling the pinch as creditors started to circle.

Static buzzed and a husky, feminine voice spoke in his ear. 'Hello?'

Yes! His instinct had been right.

'I'm here to see Madam Ruggiero.'

'Monsieur Giscard? I was expecting you. Please come up.'

Jonas pushed open the security door into a marble foyer. He ignored the lift and strode up the couple of floors to what had been his father's love nest. Suppressing a shiver of revulsion, he rapped on the door of the apartment.

It swung open almost immediately and he stepped past a slim young woman into a lavishly furnished foyer. Through an open door he glimpsed an overfull salon but no sign of the woman he'd come to see. He moved towards the inner room.

'You're not Monsieur Giscard.' The accusation halted him.

He swung round to find eyes the colour of rich sherry fixed on him.

'No. I'm not.'

For the first time he paused to survey the woman properly and something—surprise?—rushed through him.

Slim to the point of fragility, she nevertheless had curves in all the right places, even if they were obscured by ill-fitting dark clothes. But it was her face that arrested him. Wide lush mouth, strong nose, angled cheekbones that gave her a fey air, lavish dark lashes and rather straight brows framing eyes so luminous they seemed to glow. Each feature in her heart-shaped face was so definite that together they should have jarred. Instead they melded perfectly.

She was arresting. Not pretty but something much rarer. Jonas felt his pulse quicken as heat shot low in his body.

He stiffened. When was the last time the sight of a woman, even a uniquely beautiful one, had affected him?

'And you are?' She tilted her head, drawing his gaze from her ripe mouth to the ultra-short sable hair she wore like a chic, ruffled cap. Another few weeks and she'd have curls.

He frowned. Why notice that when he had more important matters on his mind?

'Looking for Madam Ruggiero. Silvia Ruggiero.' It surprised him how difficult it was to drag his gaze away and back to the apartment's inner rooms.

'You don't have an appointment.' There was something new in her voice. Something hard and flat.

'No.' His mouth curled in a smile of grim anticipation. 'But she'll see me.'

The young woman strode back into his line of sight, blocking his way to the salon. Jonas catalogued the lithe grace of her movements even as he told himself he didn't have time for distractions.

She shook her head. 'You're the last person she'd see.'

'You know who I am?' His gaze sharpened as he took in her defiant stance—arms akimbo and feet planted wide, as if she could prevent him if he chose to push past! She was tall, her mouth on a level with his collarbone, and she stared up at him with complete assurance.

'It took me a moment but of course I do.' A flicker of expression crossed her features so swiftly Jonas couldn't read it. But he watched her swallow and realised she wasn't as confident as she appeared. Interesting.

'And you are?' Jonas was used to being recognised from press reports, but instinct told him he'd met this woman before. Something about her tugged at half-buried memory.

'Forgettable, obviously.' Her lips twisted in a self-deprecating smile that ridiculously drove a spike of heat through his belly.

Jonas blinked. She wasn't smiling at him yet he reacted.

Annoyance flared. He drew himself up, watching her gaze skate across his shoulders and chest.

'She's not here.' The words tumbled out in a breathless rush that belied her aggressively protective stance. 'So you can't see her.'

'Then I'll wait.' Jonas stepped forward, only to come up against her slim frame, vibrating with tension. He'd expected her to give way. She surprised him with her determination to stand her ground. But he refused to retreat, no matter how distracting the sensation of her body against his. His business with Silvia Ruggiero was long overdue.

He looked down and her golden brown eyes widened as if in shock.

'I'm not going away,' he murmured, suppressing an inexplicable desire to lift his hand and see if her pale face was as soft as it appeared. The realisation threw him, making his voice emerge harshly. 'My business won't wait.'

Again she swallowed. He followed the movement of her slim throat with a fascination that surprised him. The scent of her skin filled his nostrils: feminine warmth and the tang of cinnamon.

Abruptly she stepped back, her chest rising and falling quickly, drawing his attention till he snapped his eyes back to her face.

'In that case you can talk with me.' She turned and led the way into the salon, her steps a clipped, staccato beat on the honey-coloured wood floor.

Jonas dragged his gaze from the sway of her hips in dark trousers and followed, furious to find himself distracted from his purpose even for a moment.

She settled herself on an overstuffed chair near a window framed by cloth of gold curtains. Hoping to put him at a disadvantage with her back to the light? It was such an obvious ploy. Instead of taking a seat Jonas prowled the room, knowing that with each passing moment her unease increased. Whoever she was, she was in cahoots with Silvia Ruggiero. Jonas wouldn't trust her an inch.

'Why should I share my business with a stranger?' He peered at an over-decorated ormolu clock.

Was there nothing in this place that wasn't overdone? It reeked of a nouveau riche fixation with show and quantity rather than quality. His cursory survey had revealed the best pieces in the room to be fakes. But that had been his father—all show and no substance. Especially when it came to things like love or loyalty.

'I'm not a stranger.' Her tone was curt. 'Perhaps if you stopped your crude inventory you'd realise that.'

To Jonas' surprise unfamiliar heat rose under his skin. True, his behaviour was crass, calculated to unnerve rather than reassure. But he felt no need to ingratiate himself with his father's mistress or her crony.

He took his time swinging around to meet her eyes.

'Then perhaps you'll do me the courtesy of answering my question. Who are you?'

'I thought that would be obvious. I'm Ravenna. Silvia's daughter.'

Ravenna watched shock freeze Jonas' features.

You'd think after all these years she'd be used to it, but still it struck her a blow.

She'd been a gawky child, all long limbs and feet and a nose it had taken years to grow into. With her dark, Italian looks, exotic name and husky voice she'd been the odd one out in her English country schools. When people saw her with her petite, ravishingly beautiful mother, the kindest comments had been about her being 'different' or 'striking'. The unkindest, at the boarding school her mother had scrimped to send her to—well, she'd put that behind her years ago.

But she'd thought Jonas would remember her, even if she'd worn braces and plaits last time they'd met.

True it had taken her a few moments to recognise him. To reconcile the grim, abrasive intruder in the exquisitely tailored clothes with the young man who'd treated her so kindly the day he'd found her curled in misery behind the stables. He'd been softer then, more understanding. To her dazed teenage eyes he'd shone like a demigod, powerful, reassuring and sexy in the unattainable way of movie stars.

Who'd have thought someone with such charm could turn into a louse?

Only the sex appeal was unchanged.

She looked again into those narrowed pewter-grey eyes that surveyed her so closely.

No, that had changed too. The softness of youth had been pared from Jonas Deveson's features, leaving them austerely sculpted and attractively spare, the product of generations of aristocratic breeding. He wasn't a chinless wonder of pampered privilege but the sort of hard-edged, born-to-authority man you could imagine defending Deveson Hall astride a warhorse, armed with sword and mace.

From his superbly arrogant nose to his strong chin, from his thick, dark hair to his wide shoulders and deep chest, Jonas was the sort to make females lose their heads.

How could she find him attractive when he oozed disapproval? When his barely veiled aggression had kept her on tenterhooks from the moment he stalked in the door?

But logic had little to do with the frisson of awareness skimming Ravenna's skin and swirling in her abdomen.

Steadily she returned his searching look. No matter how handsome he was, or how used to command, she wasn't about to fall in with his assumption of authority.

'What's your business with my mother?' Ravenna sat back, crossing one leg over the other and placing her hands on the arms of the chair as if totally relaxed.

He flicked a look from her legs to her face and she felt a prick of satisfaction that she'd surprised him. Did he expect her to bow and scrape in his presence? The thought shored up her anger.

'When will she be back?' No mistaking the banked fury in those flashing eyes. For all his outward show of calm his patience was on a short leash.

'If you can't answer politely, you might as well leave.' Ravenna shot to her feet. She had enough on her plate without dealing with Piers' privileged son. Just confronting him sapped her already low stamina. The last thing she needed was for him to guess how weak she felt. He'd just railroad her into doing his bidding—he had that look about him.

She was halfway to the door when his words stopped her.

'My business with your mother is private.'

Slowly she turned, cataloguing the harsh light in his eyes and the straight set of his mouth. Whatever his business it spelled trouble and Mamma wasn't in any state to deal with him. She was floundering, trying to adjust to the loss of the man she'd loved so ardently. Ravenna had to protect her.

'My mother's not in Paris. You can deal with me.'

He shook his head and took a pace towards her. It ate up the space between them alarmingly, bringing him within touching distance.

Did she imagine she felt the heat of his body warm her?

'Where is she?' It wasn't a request but a demand. 'Tell me now.'

Ravenna curled her fingers into tight fists, her nails scoring her flesh. His high-handed attitude infuriated her.

'I'm not your servant.' By a miracle she kept her voice even. She knew the guilt Silvia had suffered for years because of this man's refusal to reconcile with his father. 'My mother might have worked for your family once but don't think you can come here and throw your weight around. You have no power over me.'

Anger pulsed between them, so strong she felt it throb hard against her chest wall.

At least she thought it was anger. The air between them clogged with tension that stole her breath and furred the nape of her neck.

'But I do have power over your mother.' The words were silky soft, like an endearment. But it was suppressed violence she heard in that smooth baritone, a clear threat.

'What do you mean?' Alarm raised her voice an octave.

'I mean your mother's in serious trouble.'

Fear clawed at Ravenna's throat and she swallowed hard, taking in the pitiless gleam in his silvery eyes.

Understanding hit. 'You're not here to help, are you?'

His bark of laughter confirmed the icy foreboding slithering along Ravenna's spine.

'Hardly!' He paused, as if savouring the moment. 'I'm here to see she goes to prison for her crimes.'

CHAPTER TWO

RAVENNA LOCKED HER knees as the room swirled sickeningly.

She reached out a groping hand to steady herself and grabbed fabric, fingers digging claw-like as she fought panic.

The last few months had been tougher than anything she could once have imagined. They'd tested her to the limits of endurance. But nothing had prepared her to confront such pure hatred as she saw in Jonas Deveson's face. There was no softness in his expression, just adamantine determination. It scared her to the core.

Shock slammed into her and the knowledge, surer with every gasping breath, that he was serious. He intended to send her mother to prison.

A hand covered hers to the wrist, long fingers encompassing hers easily, sending darts of searing heat through her chilled flesh.

Stunned, Ravenna looked down to find she'd grabbed the only thing near—the lapel of Jonas Deveson's tailored jacket. Now he held her hard and fast.

'Are you all right?' Concern turned his deep voice to mellow treacle. She felt it softening sinew and taut muscle, easing her shocked stasis enough that she finally managed to inhale. The spinning room settled.

She tugged her hand away. Worryingly, she felt cold without that skin-to-skin contact.

Ravenna spun on her foot and paced to the window. This

time when she clutched fabric it was the heavy gold swag of curtain. It was rich and smooth under her tingling fingers, but not as reassuring as the fine wool warmed by Jonas Deveson's body.

She shook her head, banishing the absurd thought.

'Ravenna?'

Her head jerked up. She remembered him calling her by name years before, the only time they'd really talked. In her emotionally charged state then she'd imagined no one but he could ever make her name sound so appealing. For years her unusual name had been the source of countless jibes. She'd been labelled the scrawny raven and far, far worse at school. It was disturbing to discover that even now he turned her name into something special.

'What?'

'Are you okay?' His voice came from closer and she stiffened her spine.

'As okay as you can expect when you barge in here threatening my mother with gaol.'

For a moment longer Ravenna stared out of the window. The Place des Vosges, elegant and symmetrical with its manicured gardens, looked as unchanged as ever, as if nothing could disturb its self-conscious complacency.

But she'd learned the hard way that real life was never static, never safe.

Reluctantly she turned to find him looming over her, his eyes unreadable.

'What is she supposed to have done?'

'There's no *suppose* about it. Do you think I'd come *here*—' his voice was ripe with contempt as he swept the salon with a wide gesture '—if it wasn't fact?'

Ravenna's heart dropped. She couldn't believe her mother had done anything terrible, but at the same time she knew only the most extreme circumstances would bring Jonas Deveson within a kilometre of Silvia Ruggiero. There was hatred in his eyes when he spoke of her.

'You're too angry to think straight.' At her words his lowering dark brows shot up towards his hairline. Clearly this was a man unused to opposition.

She drew another, slower breath. 'You've despised my mother for years and now you think you've found a way to make her pay for the sin of falling in love with your father.'

The sizzle of fire in his eyes told her she'd hit the nail on the head. Her hands slipped onto her hips as she let righteous indignation fortify her waning strength.

'I think you've decided that, without Piers here to defend her, she's easy prey.' Her breath hitched. 'But she's not alone. You'd do well to remember that.'

'What? She's moved on already?' His voice was contemptuous. 'She's found another protector to take his place? That must be some sort of record.'

Ravenna wasn't aware of lunging towards him but suddenly she was so close she saw his pupils dilate as her open hand swung up hard and fast towards his cheek.

The movement came to a juddering halt that reverberated through her as he caught her wrist. He lifted it high so she stretched up on her toes, leaning towards him. Her breasts, belly and thighs tingled as if from an electric charge as the heat of his body, mere centimetres away, burned hers.

His eyebrows lowered, angling down straight and obstinate over eyes so intent they seemed to peer into her very soul.

His scent—clean male skin and a hint of citrus—invaded her nostrils. Abruptly she realised she'd ventured too far into dangerous territory when she found herself inhaling and holding her breath.

A shimmy of reaction jittered through her. A reaction she couldn't name. It froze the air in her lungs.

Instinct warned he was dangerous in ways that had nothing to do with her mother.

Ravenna tugged hard but he refused to release her hand. Leaning up towards him like this, almost touching along the length of their bodies, Ravenna became fully aware of the raw, masculine power hidden beneath the designer suit. The clothes were those of an urbane businessman. The burning stare and aura of charged testosterone spoke instead of primitive male power, barely leashed.

She breathed deep, trying to douse rising panic, and registered an unfamiliar spicy musk note in the air. Her nerves stretched tighter.

Never had Ravenna felt so aware of the imbalance of physical power between male and female. Of the fact that, despite her height, she was no match for this man who held her so easily and so off balance.

'Nobody slaps me.' His lips barely moved, yet Ravenna felt his warm breath on her face with each terse word.

'Nobody insults my mother like that.'

Even stretched taut against him, her mind grappling with a multitude of new sensations, she refused to back down. She stared into those glittering, merciless eyes and felt a thrill of fear, realising he was utterly unyielding.

'Then we're at an impasse, Ms Ruggiero.'

Did he tug her closer or did she sway towards him? Suddenly keeping her balance was almost impossible as she teetered on the balls of her feet.

'In which case there's no need for the macho act. You can let me go.' She paused, deliberately going limp in his hold. 'Unless you feel you have something to prove.'

Relief gushed through her as he released her.

Rather than let him see it, Ravenna bent her head as if examining her wrist for bruises. There wouldn't be any. His touch hadn't been brutal, but its implacability had scared her.

'Let's get one thing straight,' she said finally, looking up into his arresting, aristocratic face. 'My mother loved your father.'

'You expect me to believe that?' Jonas shook his head, his lips curling in a sneer. 'I'm not some callow kid who believes in fairy tales. She was on the make—out to snare a rich lover. It was obvious to everyone.' He raised a silencing hand when she would have spoken. 'She flaunted herself every chance she got.'

'My mother never—'

'He was years older, with a wife, a home, a family. He had an extraordinarily comfortable lifestyle, the respect of his peers and a social life he revelled in. You think a man of my father's disposition would give all that up unless he'd been lured into it by a clever gold-digger?'

Ravenna hesitated, as ever torn by the knowledge of how many people had been hurt by Piers and her mother. But loyalty made her speak up.

'You don't believe in love, then?'

'Love?' He almost snorted the word. 'Silvia pandered to his desires in the most obvious way. I'm sure he loved flaunting her just as he loved showing off his other possessions.' His gaze raked the room, lingering on a Cézanne on the far wall that Ravenna knew for a fact was a copy of an original sold just last year. The derisive twist of Jonas' lips told her he knew it too.

'And as for her...' Wide shoulders shrugged. 'He was just a meal ticket. They had nothing in common except a love of luxury and an aversion to hard work. Why should she toil on as a housekeeper when she could be kept in style for simply letting him—'

'That's enough!' Bile blocked Ravenna's throat and she swallowed hard, forcing it down. 'I don't want to hear any more of your poison.'

His brows rose. 'You're hardly a schoolkid any more, Ravenna.' This time when he said her name there was no lingering warmth and no frisson of subtle reaction. 'You can't pretend.'

'Leave it!' She put up her hand for silence. 'We'll never agree, so leave it.' She hefted in a deep, steadying breath. 'Just cut to the chase and tell me why you're here.'

* * *

Fury still sizzled in Jonas' blood so he took his time slowing his breathing and finding his equilibrium. It wasn't like him to lose his cool. He was known for his detachment, his calm clarity of vision even in the most potentially dangerous of commercial ventures.

And in his personal life…he'd learned his lesson early, watching his father lurch from one failed love affair to another. He'd seen the ecstatic highs of each new fixation, then the boredom and disappointment of each failure.

Jonas wasn't like his father. He'd made it his business to be as different from the old man as humanly possible. He was rock steady, reliable, controlled.

Except right now his hands shook with the force of his feelings. He swept the gilded room with a contemptuous glance and assured himself it was inevitable his father's flashy love nest would evoke a reaction.

'Well? I'm waiting.'

At her husky voice he turned to survey her.

Ravenna Ruggiero. He'd never have recognised her as the tear-stained girl he remembered. Then she'd been lanky with the coltishness of youth, her features still settling and her hair in ribbons, as if to remind him she was still a child. Only her mouth and her stunning eyes had hinted at beauty. And the low register of her voice that even then had unsettled him with its promise of sensuality to come.

It had come all right.

Silvia Ruggiero had been a stunning woman in her prime. But her daughter, even dressed in sombre, loose clothes, outshone her as a flawless diamond did a showy synthetic gem.

There was something about Ravenna. Not just a face that drew the eye as a magnet drew metal so he'd had to force himself not to stare. But an elegance, a grace, that contrasted with yet magnified the earthy sexuality of her voice, and that sassy attitude of hers…

The feel of her stretched up against him, her breasts almost grazing him as she panted her fury in defiance of his superior strength, had stirred something long dormant.

Suspended in a moment of sheer, heady excitement, he'd revelled in the proximity of her soft curves and lush mouth. There'd been a subversive pleasure in her combative attitude, in watching the sparks fly as she launched herself at him.

For the first time in his life Jonas, who preferred his pleasures planned, wondered about being on the receiving end of such unbridled passion. Not just her anger, but—

'Did you hear me?' Fingers clicked in the air before him, dragging his attention to her flushed face.

The colour suited her better, he realised, than the milky pallor he'd noticed earlier. Then he cursed himself for the stray thought.

'You want to know what your mother's been up to?' It was easy to thrust aside his unsettling distraction and focus on familiar ire. 'She's stolen money. My money.'

He had the satisfaction of seeing Ravenna's eyes widen.

It galled him that she'd had the temerity to defend Silvia when they both knew the truth about her mother. Like a magpie with an eye for a pretty, expensive bauble, she'd feathered her nest with his father's wealth.

Jonas recalled the day he'd come home unexpectedly to Deveson Hall from London and found the housekeeper in his mother's suite, in front of a mirror, holding an heirloom choker of sapphires and pearls to her throat. Instead of embarrassment at being caught out, she'd laughed and simply said no woman could have resisted the temptation if she'd found the necklace lying there. Without turning a hair she'd put it down on the dressing table and turned to plump the cushions on a nearby settee.

'No.' This time Ravenna's low voice sounded scratchy as if with shock. 'She wouldn't do that.'

'Wouldn't she?' He looked around the over-stuffed room, wondering how many of the pieces were what they appeared.

Money had obviously been tight enough for his father to cash in the more valuable pieces.

'Of course not.' Ravenna's certainty tugged his attention back to her. No longer flushed but pale and composed, she stared back with infuriating certainty.

'Then how do you explain the fact she forged my father's signature in a cheque book she shouldn't even have had access to?'

'Why blame my mother?'

'No one else had access. Piers would have kept it safely by him, believe me.' He let his gaze rove the room. 'I'm sure if we search the apartment we'll find it.'

'There'll be no searching the apartment. And even if it was here, what's to say it wasn't Piers' signature? His handwriting could have changed when he got ill.'

Jonas shook his head. 'That would have been convenient, wouldn't it? But it won't wash. Unless you can explain how he managed to cash a cheque the day after he died.'

Her eyes widened, growing huge in her taut face.

'I don't believe you.' It was a whisper but even that was like a flame to gunpowder. How could she deny her mother's wrongdoing even now?

'I don't care what you believe.' It was a lie. Her blind faith in the gold-digging Silvia was like salt on a raw wound. Perhaps because he'd never known such loyalty from his own parents. Why should she lavish it on a woman so patently undeserving?

Piers had been an absentee parent, finding plenty of reasons to stay in the city rather than at the Hall. As for his mother—he supposed she'd loved him in her own abstracted way. But she'd been more focused on her personal disappointment in marrying a man who loved not her but the wealth she'd brought with her.

Jonas slipped a hand into his jacket pocket and withdrew the photocopied cheques.

'Here.' He held them out, daring her to take them. 'I

never lie.' His father had been an expert at distorting the truth for his convenience. As a kid Jonas had vowed never to do the same.

He watched Ravenna swallow, the movement convulsive, then she reached out and took the papers. Her head bowed as she stared at them.

The sound of her breath hissing in told him he'd finally got through to her. There was no escaping the truth.

The papers moved as if in a strong breeze and he realised her hands were trembling.

In that instant guilt pierced his self-satisfaction. Belatedly it struck him that taking out his anger on Silvia's daughter was beneath him.

His belly clenched as he reviewed their encounter. Even given his determination to make Silvia pay for her crime, he'd behaved crassly. He'd stalked in, making demands when a simple request for information would have done. Worse, he'd been too caught up in own emotional turmoil to spare a thought for the shock this would be for Ravenna.

'Do you want to sit down?' The words shot out like bullets, rapid and harsh with self-disgust.

She didn't say anything, just stood, head bowed, staring at the papers in her shaking hands.

Hell! Was she in shock?

He leant towards her, trying to read her expression.

All he registered was the stiff set of her jaw and the scent of warm cinnamon and fragrant woman.

And the way she bit her bottom lip, pearly teeth sinking deep in that lush fullness.

Jonas breathed in slowly, telling himself the heat whirling in his belly was shame, not arousal.

The idea of being turned on so easily by any woman was anathema to a man who prided himself on his restraint. When she was the daughter of the woman who'd destroyed his mother... Unthinkable!

'Ravenna?' His voice sounded ridiculously hesitant, as if the ground had shifted beneath his feet.

She looked up, her eyes ablaze as they met his. Then her gaze shifted towards the window.

'You're mistaken.' Her voice sounded wrong, he realised, tight and hard. 'Silvia had nothing to do with this.'

'Stop denying, Ravenna. It's too late for that. I've got proof of her forgery.'

'Proof of forgery, yes. But not Silvia's.' She shifted, standing taller.

Jonas shook his head, weary of the unexpected emotional edge to this interview. 'Just tell me where she is and I'll deal with her.'

Those warm sherry eyes lifted to his and he stilled as he saw how they'd glazed with emotion.

'You don't need to deal with her. She had nothing to do with it.' Ravenna tilted her chin up, her gaze meeting his squarely. 'I did it. I took your money.'

CHAPTER THREE

RAVENNA'S PULSE KICKED as Jonas stiffened. Her throat dried so much it hurt to swallow. But she didn't dare turn away. Instead she met his stare unflinchingly.

She feared if she showed even a flicker of the emotions rioting inside, he wouldn't believe her.

He had to! The alternative, of pinning the theft on her mother, was untenable.

With Jonas' revelation so much fell into place—Piers' remarkable generosity in not just covering her medical costs these last months, but funding the long convalescent stay at an exorbitantly expensive Swiss health resort.

Only it hadn't been Piers making that final, massive payment, had it? It must have been Silvia—breaking the law to help her daughter.

Ravenna's heart plummeted as she recalled her mother's insistence that she needed total rest to recuperate. That without the health resort there was a danger of the treatment failing. Ravenna, too weary by then to protest when all she wanted was to rest quietly and get her strength back, hadn't put up much resistance.

She'd never sponged off Piers' wealth, and had silenced her protesting conscience by vowing to pay back every last euro. It was only when she'd arrived at the Paris apartment the other day that she realised they were euros Piers and her mother could ill afford.

Guilt had struck Ravenna when she saw how much they'd sold off. But she'd never for a moment thought her mother had purloined money that wasn't hers!

Oh, Mamma, what have you done?

Through the years Silvia had gone without again and again so Ravenna could have warm clothes and a roof over her head. And later, so she could go to the respected school her mother thought she needed. But to take what wasn't hers…!

'You're lying.' Jonas' frigid eyes raked her face and a chill skimmed her backbone.

Ravenna smoothed damp palms down her trousers and angled her chin, trying to quell the roiling nausea in her stomach.

'I don't lie.' It was true. Maybe that was why she hadn't convinced him. Her muscles clenched as desperation rose.

She couldn't let him guess the truth. Already a broken woman, Mamma would be destroyed by the shame and stress of gaol.

For a moment Ravenna toyed with blurting out the whole truth, revealing why her mother had stolen the funds and throwing them both on Jonas Deveson's mercy.

Except he didn't have any mercy.

That softer side he'd once shown her years before had been an aberration. In the six years Silvia and Piers had been together, Jonas hadn't once condescended to acknowledge his father's existence. He had ice in his veins rather than warm blood, and a predilection for holding a grudge.

Now it seemed he had a taste for vengeance too.

That might be ice in his veins but there was fire blazing in his eyes. It had been there since he shouldered his way into the apartment, prowling the room with lofty condescension as if his father's death meant nothing to him.

His hatred for her mother was a palpable weight in the charged atmosphere.

He blamed Silvia for his father's defection. He'd sided

with the rest of his aristocratic connections in shunning the working-class foreigner who'd had the temerity to poach one of their own.

Ravenna had to keep this from her. If Mamma found the theft had been discovered she'd come forward and accept the penalty. Ravenna couldn't let her do that, not when she saw the violence in Jonas Deveson's eyes. She couldn't condone what Mamma had done but could understand it, especially since she must have been overwrought about Piers.

'You haven't got it in you to do that, Ravenna.' He shook his head. 'Theft is more your mother's style.'

Fury boiled in her bloodstream. She didn't know which was worse, his bone-deep hatred of her mother or that he thought he knew either of them when at Deveson Hall family hadn't mixed with staff.

His certainty of her innocence should have appeased her; instead, tainted as it was by prejudice, Ravenna found herself angrier than she could ever remember. Rage steamed across her skin and seeped from her pores.

'You have no idea of what her style is or mine.' Her teeth gritted around the words.

His damnably supercilious eyebrows rose again. 'I'm a good judge of character.'

That was what Ravenna feared. That was why she had to work hard to convince him.

Maybe if her mother had a spotless reputation she'd ride out a trial with nothing worse than a caution and community service. But sadly that wasn't the case.

Years before, when Silvia had been young and homeless, kicked out by her father for shaming the family with her pregnancy, she'd resorted to shoplifting to feed herself. She'd been tried then released on a good behaviour bond. That had terrified the young woman who'd been until then completely law abiding.

Much later, when Ravenna was nine, her mother had been accused of stealing from the house where she worked.

Ravenna remembered Mamma's ravaged, parchment-white face as the police led her away under the critical gaze of the woman who employed her. It didn't matter that the charges had been dropped when the woman's daughter was found trying to sell the missing heirloom pieces. Silvia had been dismissed, presumably because her employer couldn't face the embarrassment of having accused an innocent woman.

Mud stuck and innocence didn't seem to matter in the face of prejudice.

Look at the way Jonas already judged her. If she went to trial he'd dredge up her past and every scurrilous innuendo he could uncover and probably create a few for good measure. His air of ruthlessness that chilled Ravenna. His lawyers would make mincemeat out of her mother.

Ravenna couldn't allow it. Especially since her mother had stolen to save her.

Hot guilt flooded her. How desperate Mamma must have been, how worried, to have stolen this man's money! She must have known he'd destroy her if he found out.

Which was why Ravenna had to act.

She stepped forward, her index finger prodding Jonas' hard chest. It felt frighteningly immovable. But she had to puncture his certainty. Attack seemed her best chance.

'Don't pretend to know my mother.' Furtively she sucked in air, her breathing awry as her pulse catapulted. 'You weren't even living at home when we moved to Deveson Hall.'

'You're telling me you masterminded this theft?' His tone was sceptical. 'I think not.'

'You—' her finger poked again '—aren't in a position to know anything about me.'

'Oh, I wouldn't say that.' Warm fingers closed around her hand so that suddenly she was no longer the aggressor but his captive. Tendrils of sensation curled up her arm and made her shiver. 'I know quite a bit about you. I know you hated school, especially maths and science. You wanted to run away but felt you had to stick it out for your mother's sake.'

Ravenna's eyes widened. 'You remember that?' Her voice faded to a whisper. She'd assumed he'd long forgotten her teary confession the day he'd found her wallowing in teenage self-pity.

'You hated being made to play basketball just because you were tall. As I recall you wanted to be tiny, blonde and one of five children, all rejoicing in the name of Smith.'

It was true. Living up to her mother's expectations of academic and social success had been impossible, especially for an undistinguished scholar like Ravenna, surrounded by unsupportive peers who treated her as a perennial outsider. For years she'd longed, not to be 'special' but to blend in.

'And you didn't like the way one of the gardeners had begun to stare at you.'

Ridiculously heat flushed her skin. That summer she'd been a misfit, neither child nor adult. She hadn't known what she wanted.

But she hadn't minded when Jonas Deveson looked at her or, for one precious, fleeting moment, stroked wayward curls off her face.

Ravenna blinked. She wasn't fifteen now.

'You remember far more of that day than I do.' Another lie. Two in one day had to be a record for her. Maybe if she kept it up she could even sound convincing.

Did she imagine a slight softening in those grey eyes?

No. Easier to believe she'd scored her dream job as a pastry chef in a Michelin-starred restaurant than that this steely man had a compassionate side.

'You haven't changed that much.' His deep voice stirred something unsettling deep inside.

'No? You didn't even recognise me.' She pulled back but he didn't loosen his grip. He held her trapped.

For a moment fear spidered through her, till she reminded herself he had too much pride to force himself on an unwilling woman. His hold wasn't sexual, it was all about power. The charged awareness was all on her side, not his.

She had no intention of analysing that. She had enough to worry about.

'You've changed a lot.' Her tone made it clear it wasn't a compliment. At twenty-one he'd been devastatingly handsome but unexpectedly kind and patient. She'd liked him, even more than liked him in her naïve way.

Now he was all harsh edges, irascible and judgemental. What was there to like?

'We're not here to discuss me.' His eyes searched hers. Stoically she kept her head up and face blank. Better to brazen out her claim than show a hint of doubt.

Yet inside she was wobbly as jelly. The past days had taken their toll as she saw how grief had ravaged her mother, making her seem frail. Ravenna had sent her away from the apartment so ripe with memories of Piers. She'd offered to pack up the flat and deal with the landlord, but even those simple tasks were a test of Ravenna's endurance. Now this…

'We're here to discuss my money.' Jonas' fingers firmed around her. 'The money stolen from my account.'

Ravenna swallowed hard at his unrelenting tone.

Just what *was* the penalty for theft and forgery?

Jonas felt her hand twitch in his.

A sign of guilt or proof she lied about being the one who'd ripped him off?

Her soft eyes were huge in her finely sculpted face, giving her an air of fragility despite her punk-short hair and belligerently angled chin.

Jonas wasn't sentimental enough to let looks mar his decision-making. Yet, absurdly, he found himself hesitating.

He didn't *want* to believe Ravenna guilty.

Far easier to believe her rapacious mother had organised this swindle. After years keeping his emotions bottled up he'd almost enjoyed the roaring surge of fury against his father's mistress that had borne him across the channel in a red-misted haze.

But what bothered him most was the recognition he didn't want it to be Ravenna because he remembered her devastating innocence and honesty years ago. He didn't want to reconcile that memory with the knowledge she'd become a thief.

Jonas' lips twisted. Who'd have thought he still had illusions he didn't want to shatter? He'd been too long in the cut-throat business world to believe in the innate honesty of mankind. Experience had taught him man—and womankind were out for all they could get.

Why should this revelation be so unwelcome?

'You say you wrote the cheques?'

Again that jerk of tension through her. Her pulse tripped against his palm and he resisted the absurd impulse to caress her there.

She nodded, the movement brief but emphatic.

'How did you get access to the cheque book?' Piers would have been canny enough to keep it close at hand, not lying around. 'Were you living here with them?'

'No, I—' She paused and her gaze shifted away. Instinct told him she hid something. 'But I visited. Often. My mother and I have always been close.'

That at least had the ring of truth. He remembered her misery in her teens, not simply because she hated school and the vicious little witches who made her life hell there, but because she didn't want to disappoint her mother by leaving. She cared what her mother thought.

Enough to learn her mother's ways in seeking easy money from a man? Had she modelled herself on Silvia?

The notion left a sour tang of disappointment on his tongue.

'You're hurting me!'

Jonas eased his grip, but didn't let her go. He was determined to sort this out. Until then he'd keep her close.

'Why did you need the money?'

Her eyebrows arched and she tilted her head as if to inspect him. As if he weren't already close enough to see the rays of gold in the depths of her eyes.

'You're kidding, right?' Her tone of insouciant boredom echoed the attitude of entitlement he'd heard so often among wealthy, privileged young things who'd never worked a day in their lives. Except something in her tone was ever so slightly off-key.

Suspicion snaked through him.

He pulled her closer, till her body mirrored his. He felt the tension hum through her. Good! He wanted her unsettled.

'A girl needs to live, doesn't she?' This time there was an edge of desperation in her tone. 'I've had...expenses.'

'What sort of expenses? Even shopping at the top Parisian fashion houses wouldn't have swallowed up all that money.'

Her gaze slid from his. 'This and that.'

A cold, hard weight formed in the pit of Jonas' belly. He was surprised to feel nausea well.

'Drugs?'

She shook her head once, then shrugged. 'Debts.'

'Gambling?'

'Why the inquisition? I've admitted I took your money. That's all that matters.' Her gaze meshed with his and a jagged flash of heat resonated through Jonas. It stunned him.

How could a mere look do that? It wasn't even a sultry invitation but a surly, combative stare that annoyed the hell out of him.

Yet aftershocks still tumbled through his clenching belly and he found himself leaning closer, inhaling her warm cinnamon and hot woman scent.

This couldn't be happening.

He refused to feel anything for the woman who'd stolen from him. Especially since she was Silvia Ruggiero's daughter. The thought of that family connection was like a cold douche.

Deliberately he chose his next words to banish any illusion of closeness. 'Why steal from me when Piers would have indulged a pretty young thing like you? I'm sure he'd have been amendable to *private* persuasion.'

'You're sick. You know that? Piers was with my *mother*. He had no interest in me.' She drew herself up as if horrified. Either she was a brilliant actor or she drew the line at men old enough to be her father.

'In my experience he wasn't discriminating.'

Ravenna yanked her hand to free it from his grasp but Jonas wasn't playing. He wrapped his other arm hard around her narrow back, drawing her up against him.

Just to keep her still, he assured himself.

It worked. With a stifled gasp she froze. Only the quick rise and fall of her breasts against his arm where he still held her hand revealed animation.

'Speaking from personal experience, are you, Jonas?' Her voice was all sneer. 'What are you doing now? Copping a feel?'

His jaw ached with the effort to bite back a retort.

Unlike his father he'd never been a sucker for a pretty face and a show of cleavage. Sure, he appreciated a sexy woman. But he was discriminating, private in his affairs and loyal to whomever he was with. His intellect and his sense of honour took precedence over cheap thrills.

When he married there'd be no shady liaisons on the side, no whispered rumours and knowing looks to embarrass his family. None of the pain to which Piers had subjected them.

Jonas stared down at the firebrand who'd managed to tap into emotions he'd kept safely stowed for years. In one short interlude she'd cut through years of hard-won self-control so he teetered on the brink of spontaneous, uncharacteristic, dangerous action. He almost growled his fury and frustration aloud.

He wanted to lean down and silence her sassy mouth, force those lush lips apart and relieve some of his frustrated temper in steamy passion and a vibrant, accommodating woman.

She'd be receptive, despite that accusatory look. That was what made the idea so tempting. Ravenna might hate him for making her face what she'd done. But it wasn't merely anger she felt for him—not by a long chalk.

'Oh, I choose my women very carefully, Ravenna.' His voice was a low, guttural burr. 'And I never take anything from a woman that's not offered freely.'

Dark satisfaction flared as he assessed her reaction with a knowing eye.

He read her rapid breathing and the flush that began at her cleavage and highlighted her cheeks. The way her tongue furtively slicked her lower lip. The indefinable scent of feminine arousal.

'Really?' Her breathless challenge didn't convince. 'Well, keep that in mind. I'm not offering you anything.'

Jonas was torn between wanting to kiss her senseless and wanting to put her over his knee. He leaned in a fraction and heard her soft exhale of breath. A sigh...of surrender or triumph?

Suddenly it hit him anew that he was in danger of succumbing to the allure of a Ruggiero female. Of an unprincipled thief who threw her crime in his teeth.

Who enticed with her soft body and tell-tale physical signals.

'Is that so?' he murmured, knowing he had her measure.

She'd use any tactic to thwart his retribution. Did she aim to play him for an easy mark, as her mother had targeted Piers?

The realisation stilled his impetuous need to taste her. Yet he couldn't draw back. He was trapped by a hunger sharper and more potent than he'd known in years.

That infuriated him even more than the missing money. He burned with it, the fire in his belly white hot with a virulent mix of lust and self-disgust at his weakness.

Keeping one arm around her back, he released her hand and let his fingers drift. She didn't flinch, didn't move, her eyes daring him to do his worst. Because she thought herself immune or because she assumed he wouldn't rise to her challenge?

His fingers brushed her soft, high breast and moulded automatically to that sweet ripeness. The hard nub of her nipple pressed into his palm and arousal seared his groin. A spasm of something like electricity jerked through his body.

For a breath-stealing moment she stood rigid as if about to lambast him for groping. Her eyes widened in shock, then dropped in heavy-lidded invitation. Her lips parted on a silent sigh. A moment later she shifted, melting against him.

'Tell me to stop and I will.'

He prayed she wouldn't.

She opened her mouth but no sound emerged.

The weight of her in his palm, the press of her body, the heady sense of promise thickening the air between them, sapped his resolution.

He was ready to take her up on her unspoken invitation. His body was rock hard with a hunger that was all the stronger for being unexpected. Why not take a little something for himself after she'd taken so much from him? Clearly she expected it, wanted it, if the tremors in her pliant body were any indication.

But that smacked of history repeating itself. The little thief would think he kept his brain between his legs, as his father had when he'd run off with her mother, leaving his responsibilities behind.

Jonas couldn't let Ravenna enjoy the illusion of triumph. He had too much pride.

He was nobody's gullible mark.

As she'd learn to her cost.

Gently he squeezed her breast, just enough to elicit a delicate shudder in her fine-boned body and a throaty sigh of delight.

The hairs on his arms prickled and his blood rushed south at the sound of her pleasure. But he refused to respond to the urges of his suddenly intemperate body.

'You like that, do you, Ravenna?'

Slitted now, her eyes had a glazed look that told its own story. She swallowed convulsively, drawing his attention to the slim length of her pale throat. The collar of her dark jacket sat loose, giving her an air of fragility at odds with the pulse of vibrant life he felt as she arched against him.

He'd pull back soon. In a moment. When he'd allowed himself a single taste...

Cinnamon and feminine spice filled his nostrils as he dipped his head, nudging aside her collar and nipping gently at the sensitive spot where her neck and shoulder met. She shook in his hold, her hand grasping his between them as if for support.

'No. Please I—'

Her words cut abruptly as Jonas laved the spot, drawing in the sweet taste of her warm skin.

Too late he realised his error, as he angled his head hungrily for a better taste, pressing kisses up her arching throat, past the throbbing pulse to the neat angle of her jaw.

She was addictive. Scent or taste or the feel of silky soft flesh, or perhaps all three, had Jonas ignoring the voice of reason and losing himself in the moment. In the luxury of caressing Ravenna.

He'd never come across a woman who tempted him so easily.

Her free hand cupped his neck, holding him close, and he pulled her tight against him, enjoying the slide of her body as she bowed back to give him free rein.

He stroked his tongue along the scented skin behind her ear and had to tighten his hold when she slumped against him as if her knees had given way.

She was so responsive, inciting a surge of arousal that swamped all else. Blood roared in his veins, primal instinct taking over. His focus blurred, his mind racing frantically with the practicalities of getting her horizontal as soon as possible.

He nipped lightly at her ear lobe and she turned her head restlessly as if seeking his lips.

Triumph hummed through him as he pressed a kiss to the corner of her lush mouth.

One quick taste then he'd find that preposterous gilded sofa and treat them both to sexual release so intense it would shatter them. Already he was hard as a rock. Carrying her across the room would be torture but he wasn't letting her go till he'd had his fill. Till they were both limp and the urgent hunger gnawing at his vitals was appeased.

His ears rang with the force of his blood rushing. He ignored it and tilted his head to take her mouth.

Except her eyes were open now and that dreamy expression had faded. Stark horror flared instead in those dark gold depths.

Jonas frowned. She wanted him. He knew it. He felt it with every muscle and sinew as she pressed herself against him. Yet—

The ringing sounded again. This time he realised it came from somewhere outside his head—the front door.

'Let me go.' Her voice was so hoarse he read her lips rather than heard her. Jonas blinked, trying to make sense of the abrupt shift in mood.

She pushed against him with both hands. 'I said, let me go!' Her gaze slid from his as if she couldn't bear to look at him. Because he'd made her forget her little game of temptation? Because she'd been the victim of unexpected lust this time instead of the temptress?

Something soured his belly. Memory. Disillusionment. The realisation that despite his vaunted immunity he'd fallen hard and fast for what she offered: hot sex with a gold-digging opportunist.

Just like his father before him.

He released her so quickly she wobbled and he reached out a hand to steady her.

'Saved by the bell,' he murmured and watched heat flush her cheeks. Not for the life of him would he let her see how she'd knocked him for six. That was his private shame.

She knocked his hand away, rubbing her palm over the place he'd held her as if to erase his touch. But he wasn't fooled by her show of antipathy. She'd lost control too. It was that latter truth that cut him to the core, tapping the long-dammed reservoir of fury so it finally broke free.

He watched her spin away from him, her steps uneven as she headed for the foyer. With each step he cursed himself for his weakness. He'd seen what she was. She'd *told* him. Yet he hadn't been able to resist her.

'If that was you being unaffected,' he drawled, 'I look forward to seeing what you're like when you put a little effort into sex.' He drew a slow breath, watching her stumble to a halt. 'I was willing to test the waters to see how far you'd go. And I wasn't disappointed.'

Her shoulders hunched but she didn't turn around.

For a moment something like sympathy hovered. Jonas had a ridiculous urge to cross the room and pull her close to comfort her.

He shook his head.

What was it about Ravenna Ruggiero that got under his skin despite what she'd done?

Was there a family weakness after all? Something in the Deveson genes that made them putty in the grasping hands of the Ruggiero women?

He gritted his teeth against a howl of fury and, worse, disappointment that now he'd never have her in his arms again. He couldn't trust himself with her. How sick was that?

He buried the knowledge behind a wall of disdain.

'Do let me know, if you decide you have something to offer me after all. I might even consider being a little less *discriminating* just for the novelty of it.'

CHAPTER FOUR

RAVENNA STARED AT the mellow wood of the floor, wishing the old boards would part in a yawning void and suck her away into nothingness. Anything to escape the sarcastic lash of Jonas Deveson's contempt.

As if she should be so fortunate! This past year there'd been no good luck in her life. Except the unexpected gift of the rest cure in Switzerland. But now it turned out that had an awful catch. An enormous debt to be paid.

And a big, ruthless debt collector to make sure she paid in blood.

She shivered, cold to the bone, yet her skin crawled with a clammy heat that matched the nausea twisting her insides. She fought it, refusing to be ill in front of him.

Could anything be more humiliating than this?

She felt sullied by him. It was far worse than facing a dressing-down by the head chef at work, whose explosive tirades were legend. As for the torments of her school years—they'd been nothing to this excruciating shame.

For this time every word was deserved. She'd behaved like some slut, eager for the touch of a man who despised her. For the first time she hadn't behaved like the sensible, careful, self-contained woman she was.

She'd acted like a hormone-riddled stranger with no scruples or self-respect.

The doorbell rang again and she dragged herself into the

foyer, propping herself against the wall with a shaking hand as she pressed the intercom.

'Monsieur Giscard?' The words were so faint she cleared her throat to try again. The response from below was garbled in ears that still thrummed with the pulse of arousal.

Nevertheless, she pressed the button to let the visitor in downstairs. Whoever it was, he couldn't be more devastating than Jonas Deveson.

She felt his eyes on her. Her skin prickled and heat drilled her spine. She could pinpoint the exact place between her shoulder blades where that penetrating gaze scored her. If she found later that his laser-sharp gaze had scorched a hole in her jacket she wouldn't be surprised.

Ravenna struggled to swallow the hard knot of emotion blocking her throat.

What had got into her to behave so utterly out of character?

Taking a deep breath, she tried to centre herself but instead inhaled the remnants of his tangy, hot citrus scent. It had impregnated her very pores.

Never in her life had attraction been like that—instantaneous and absolute. Consciously, to her thinking mind, there'd been no attraction—just fear and shock at his revelations, and a determination to divert his thunderous anger from her mother.

But something had happened when he'd touched her. Something unheralded.

She'd heard of animal attraction. She had some experience of desire.

But this… This had been a tsunami obliterating reason and doubt and anything like resistance. She'd stood like a rabbit spotlighted by a hunter, watching his eyes cloud with desire as he touched her. Excitement had stormed through her.

Part of her brain had screamed for her to move, to slap his hand away, but she'd stood, rooted to the spot, eager for more. When he'd bitten her neck in that delicate tasting, she'd gone up in flames.

How was it possible?

Brushing off male attention had never been hard. Yet she'd practically begged for more from him as carnal heat melted her insides and left her a quivering, pathetic wreck.

Where was her backbone? Her sense of self-preservation?

The doorbell rang and she stumbled forward. Her legs felt like melted wax and she fumbled at the door with shaking hands.

On the threshold stood a man of middle years, exquisitely dressed and sporting a rosebud in his lapel.

'Mademoiselle Ruggiero?' He pronounced her name with the softened consonants of the French.

'Monsieur Giscard.' She held out her hand. 'It's a pleasure to meet you. I appreciate you coming so quickly.' She led him into the apartment, carefully keeping her gaze from the far side of the salon and Jonas' watchful presence.

If she could she'd eject him from the premises, but he wouldn't leave till he was good and ready. They had too much to discuss.

At least having the antiques expert here gave her something else to concentrate on, and a chance to regroup after that devastating embrace.

Despite her best intentions her gaze slid across the room to lock with eyes the colour of impenetrable mist. Jonas' face was blank but his words echoed in her ears, making heat scorch her throat and cheeks.

Beside her the dapper Frenchman started forward eagerly, his arm outstretched as he introduced himself to Jonas Deveson. For a moment Ravenna thought the two must have met before but it appeared Monsieur Giscard simply recognised him from press reports.

Ravenna spun away on the ball of her foot. Jonas Deveson even managed to usurp the position of authority now, without trying. Her visitor was fawning over him like a long-lost son. Or a wealthy potential client.

'I have an inventory of furnishings here, Monsieur Giscard.' Reluctantly he turned towards her, and then nodded.

'Perhaps, Mr Deveson, we could meet later today to conclude our discussion?' She had a snowball's chance in hell of fobbing him off but she had to try. The idea of him watching them trail around the apartment, sizing up her mamma's possessions, made her skin crawl.

'I think not, Ravenna.' He deliberately dropped his voice to a pseudo caress on her name. To her consternation and shame she felt her skin tingle and her nipples harden.

It was as if she were programmed to respond sexually even to the cadence of his voice!

'I'm afraid Monsieur Giscard and I will be busy for some time—'

'Don't let me disturb you.' His open wave of the arm, as if graciously giving them permission to continue, made her grit her teeth. 'I'm happy to wait.'

As if to emphasise his point he sank onto a gilded chair and nonchalantly crossed his legs, his hands palm down on the arms in a pose that screamed authority. His tall frame in that delicate chair should have looked ridiculous. Instead he looked…regal.

For a second Ravenna toyed with the idea of calling for the police to eject him as an unwanted intruder. Until she realised the police were the last people she wanted. Her mother's crime loomed over her like a leaden storm cloud.

Fear sank talons deep into her vitals. This impossible situation could only get worse, given this man's implacable thirst for vengeance. Her body stiffened, adrenalin surging and heart pounding in an unstoppable fight-or-flight response. Chaotic thoughts of disappearing out of the front door and not coming back raced through her brain.

But she couldn't do it.

Ravenna was hardworking, dutiful, responsible. It was

the way she was made, reinforced no doubt by watching her mother slave so long and hard to support them both.

Besides, if she disappeared, Jonas would go after Mamma.

Drawing a slow breath, she squared her shoulders. If there was one thing the last months had taught her it was that she had the power to endure more than she'd ever thought possible. She'd pay the debt somehow, save her mother from his destructive fury, then get on with her life.

'As you wish. Feel free to make yourself comfortable.' She shot him a dazzling smile and had the momentary pleasure of seeing him disconcerted. Then she turned to Monsieur Giscard, gesturing for him to precede her from the room. 'I thought we might start in the study.'

Why Piers had needed a study was beyond Jonas. The old man hadn't worked for years, merely living off what was left of his investments.

Jonas had been at the helm of what had begun as a Deveson family investment company. He'd cut the old man from his life and manoeuvred him from the business when he'd left and destroyed Jonas' mother, never once expressing regret.

Shifting in the uncomfortable chair, he cast a scathing look around the room. It didn't improve with familiarity. The few good pieces were overwhelmed by the clutter of showy ornamentation.

Piers had been a magpie, attracted by the bright and shiny, displaying his wealth in the most obvious way. That went especially for women.

Jonas raked his hand through his hair. Had Ravenna Ruggiero's dismay been genuine when he'd suggested she should have used her feminine wiles to get money from Piers?

More important—what on earth had possessed him to touch her?

He was appalled by his reaction to her, but fascinated. He

couldn't remember being fascinated by anything other than an exciting investment opportunity in years.

Jonas shot to his feet, unwilling to sit on the sidelines.

He found them in a large room dominated by a massive desk. They were examining ornate snuffboxes.

'This is a passably good piece. You might manage a hundred euros for it.'

The antique dealer, Giscard, had his back to the door so Jonas couldn't see what he held. But Ravenna's disappointment at the words was clear. Her shoulders slumped and her whole body sagged.

'Really? I'd thought perhaps this at least might be worth more.' Her voice had an edge of desperation.

Giscard turned and Jonas watched him hesitate, his brisk manner softening as he took in her barely concealed distress.

'Well, perhaps a little more. I tend to err on the side of caution, Mademoiselle Ruggiero.' He turned back to the item in his hands. 'After a closer look I think it possible we could do better. If you like I can undertake the sale personally. I have some contacts who might be interested.'

'Really?' Ravenna's eyes shone hopefully and she leaned towards him. 'That would be wonderful, Monsieur Giscard.' Her voice was soft with hope and Jonas felt his skin contract as if she'd brushed her fingertips over him.

He clenched his jaw, furious yet intrigued at the power of that throaty voice.

'It is the least I can do in the sad circumstances.' The dealer moved closer as if drawn by her tremulous smile. 'Perhaps, in the circumstances, you should call me Etienne.'

Jonas' grip tightened on the doorjamb as the pair continued their conversation, oblivious to his presence.

Distaste was a pungent note on his tongue as he watched the older man respond to Ravenna's artful show of vulnerability. That was what it was, he realised, his lips thinning in a grim smile.

The woman who'd made such a point of confronting him

with her crime was no innocent. She was brazen and un-repentant.

From the moment she'd revealed her identity, flouncing about the astronomically expensive apartment as if it were hers, he'd wondered why she'd dressed as she had. The dark trouser suit was tailored but it hung on her, making her look like a child dressing up, especially with the gamine haircut accentuating her exquisitely pared features and huge eyes.

There'd been nothing childlike about her when he'd caressed her. She'd been all needy woman. Yet with her navy jacket hanging loose around her neck, she exuded an air of fragility that intrigued him.

Now he knew why. That vulnerability, enhanced by the sedate cut of clothes that hinted at mourning, was a deliberate act to aid her dealings with the antique dealer.

Look at Giscard! He ate her up with his eyes, like a dog slavering after a bone.

She'd prepared carefully for the interview to play on the Frenchman's sympathies.

And Jonas had doubted she was capable of thieving!

She was as conniving and dangerous as her mother.

More so. He remembered Silvia as having a blatant sensuality that made her stand out like a Mediterranean sex goddess with her flashing eyes, swinging hips and earthy laugh. But her daughter… He narrowed his eyes as he watched the woman so easily manipulating the Frenchman. She had an arresting face, the sort of eyes that a less pragmatic man could lose himself in, and a body that, though slim, made him want to haul her close and discover its secrets.

But there was more. An aura of banked passion and quick intelligence that melded into something that drew him at the most primitive, male level.

He wanted her.

The realisation hit him a solid blow to the belly.

He didn't like or admire her. She was the sort of woman he'd learnt to despise.

And still he wanted her.

He dragged in a deep breath, ignoring the anticipation fizzing his blood at the thought of bedding Ravenna Ruggiero.

It wasn't going to happen. His standards were higher than that.

Instead he would make her pay for what she'd done. He'd make sure she learned the value of the money she'd taken, and when he'd finished with her she'd understand the value of hard work too. She'd repay her debt in full. There'd be no easy escape if she tried batting those long eyelashes at him.

There'd be no police, no trial. He'd looked forward to branding his father's mistress publicly as a thief. But for reasons he didn't want to investigate, that didn't seem appropriate now Ravenna had revealed herself as the culprit.

Yes, he could throw her to the mercy of the courts. But having seen her, touched her, he wanted a much more personal recompense.

She'd stolen his money but the insult carved deeper than the loss of mere money, which, after all, was easily replaced.

Jonas told himself his decision had nothing to do with the heat haze of desire still drenching his skin as he watched her flirt with another man.

Or the feeling she'd somehow bested him in their first confrontation even though he held all the winning cards in this contest.

For there *was* a contest. Of wills. Of strength and, above all, of pride.

Somehow she'd breached the fortress he'd long ago built around his emotions. He was disappointed to discover she'd gone the way of her mother, intent on easy money rather than working for it like any decent woman. He'd expected better of her. It was as if she'd betrayed his memory of her.

His lips twisted as he reviewed his decision to give her a chance to avoid a criminal record. It was almost altruistic of him. Facing the consequences of her crime in the form of hard work might be the making of her.

Jonas' eyes narrowed as she batted those lush lashes at the besotted Frenchman. Something cold and sharp solidified in his belly.

No matter what the outcome, he looked forward to collecting on his debt.

'Now these,' purred Monsieur Giscard, 'are in a different class altogether.' He stood in front of a cabinet displaying a collection of old glassware.

'Really?' Ravenna stepped closer, her hopes rising. So far they'd come across little that could be sold to pay off Mamma's debts, let alone set her up with a nest egg for the future. 'You think they may be valuable?'

She had little expectation of finding anything to cover the money her mother had taken from Jonas Deveson's account but scraping together enough to pay Mamma's immediate bills would be an enormous relief.

'I need to examine them properly, but this appears to be a fine collection of early glassware.' He paused, excitement lighting his face. 'Really, a very fine collection...' His voice trailed as he bent to view a goblet with a long, thick stem of twisted glass.

Ravenna held her breath as he opened the cabinet and reached for the goblet.

'I'm afraid those pieces aren't for sale.' The deep voice came from just behind her and she jumped. She hadn't heard Jonas Deveson approach.

'Do you have to sneak up like that?' As soon as the words snapped out she regretted them, seeing his raised brows and knowing smirk. Maybe it was petty given the enormity of what lay between them, but she'd rather not reveal how thoroughly he unsettled her.

He didn't answer, instead turning to Monsieur Giscard, who held the glass cradled reverentially in his hands.

'C'est magnifique!'

'It is, isn't it?' Before Ravenna could stop him Jonas reached out and took it from the Frenchman, holding it up to the light for a moment, before putting it back in the cabinet and shutting the door. 'But it's not for sale.'

'Now look here—!'

He cut her off as if she hadn't spoken. 'It seems this inventory of yours is flawed.' He took the clipboard from her and glanced down at it. Before Ravenna had the presence of mind to snatch it back he'd taken a gold pen from a pocket and begun slashing lines through her list.

'You'll find the contents of this cabinet are old family pieces. They belong to my father's estate—in other words, to me.' He looked up, his silver gaze skewering her. 'Unless you'd like to try stealing this as well?'

Ravenna's breath hissed in and blood scalded her cheeks. In her peripheral vision she was aware of Monsieur Giscard's sharp, curious look.

'I didn't—'

'No?' Jonas' mouth curled up in a superior smile she'd give anything to wipe away.

'No. And it's strange that your father's solicitor hasn't been in contact about collecting anything entailed. I understood the furnishings belong to my mother.'

'Who is conveniently not here.' His voice was velvet with a razor-sharp edge. 'And who was conveniently not available when lawyers tried to contact her.'

Ravenna shook her head, denying his implied accusation. 'She's upset, grieving. She wasn't ready to handle this.'

'Which is why she installed you with your special…*capabilities,* to wrap up the estate?'

The air between them thickened and Ravenna felt fire spark in her blood. He spoke so contemptuously, as if she were a conniving thief.

Which is exactly what you want him to believe. For your mother's sake.

Caution battled fury as she swallowed a furious protest. She was battered by the intensity of his disapproval, and her need to submit.

Finally she broke eye contact and looked away. Instantly her cramped lungs eased as she sucked in sustaining oxygen.

'Monsieur Giscard.' She turned to the dealer with an apologetic smile she hoped masked her desperation. 'As you see things are not as clear cut as I'd thought. Would you mind—?'

'Of course, *mademoiselle*.' He looked only too happy to go, glancing nervously at Jonas who stood glowering like a disapproving idol, his face carved from unforgiving granite.

'I'll call you when I've sorted this out.'

'Of course, of course.' The Frenchman almost scurried out of the door and he didn't meet her eyes when she farewelled him at the entrance to the apartment.

Ravenna's skin crawled with embarrassment, reliving that moment when Jonas had spoken with such calculated cruelty about her stealing. Her stomach plummeted and she leaned against the wall for support. She'd have to get used to it if she was going to carry this off. She had a disturbing feeling it wasn't just public humiliation Jonas Deveson had planned.

He wanted more. He wanted his pound of flesh.

She shivered, remembering his strong teeth nipping at the erogenous zone in her neck. And that she'd done nothing to stop him.

'Alone at last.' His low voice curled around her like a phantom and wholly misleading caress. She should have guessed he wouldn't let her out of his sight.

Ravenna didn't bother replying. Nor did she have any intention of meeting those judgemental eyes. She turned abruptly and walked away.

'Where are you going?' His tone sharpened in surprise. Obviously he wasn't used to anyone turning their back on him.

'I need a drink.'

Of course he followed her and even in the spacious kitchen she felt that claustrophobic sense of the air thickening. She had the unnerving suspicion that even beneath a wide blue sky she'd feel hemmed in by what Jonas made her feel.

Refusing to acknowledge her burgeoning panic, she busied herself filling the kettle and getting out the cafetière.

'How very domestic.'

She shrugged. 'Well, I *am* the housekeeper's daughter.' She filled the coffee grinder and vented her feelings cranking the old-fashioned grinder.

It didn't make her feel any better.

'So, Jonas. What are your plans? Have you called the police? Am I going to be led off in handcuffs?' Her voice was so brittle the words came out in hard little bites.

'The scenario does have a certain charm.'

Ravenna stiffened, the hairs on her arms rising as she paused in the act of emptying the grinder.

'But?' There was a but in there. At least she hoped there was. Unable to pretend indifference any longer, she swung round. Predictably he lounged against the doorjamb, filling the one and only exit with his broad shoulders and athletic frame.

Ravenna licked her lips as her mouth dried. Fear rather than pride prompted her next words. 'I'll pay you back. I promise.'

'You promise?' He paused as if considering. 'And how will you do that?' He straightened and prowled across the room. She had nowhere to go and stood her ground, but the countertop bit into her back as the space between them closed. 'I'm curious. Do you have a job?'

She opened her mouth to confirm she had, then snapped it shut. She'd been a junior in the restaurant, had only worked there a few months. She'd lost her job when it became obvious she'd need months off work and that she might never return.

'No. I don't have a job at the moment.'

'Somehow that doesn't surprise me.'

'And so?' She refused to be baited. 'What are your plans?'

For the space of four heartbeats he said nothing, then his mouth turned up in a smile that didn't meet his eyes. It made him look lethally dangerous, and, to Ravenna's horror, sexy with it. If you were a woman who liked to live on a knife edge of peril. She told herself she didn't.

'Plans?' He paused. 'Oh, you mean about the theft?'

She clenched her hands. She wouldn't take another swing at him, no matter how tempted. She had no intention of getting close enough again to touch him. 'The arch air of disingenuousness doesn't suit you.'

He shrugged. 'And the wide-eyed air of innocence doesn't suit you.'

She crossed her arms so he wouldn't see how they shook. Behind her the kettle whistled and stopped but she fixed her attention on the man who held her future in his hands.

'I intend to ensure you pay back your debt. It's that simple.'

'Nothing with you is simple.'

This time there was a flicker of appreciation in his smile. 'Ah, you're a quick learner.'

When she said nothing he finally continued. 'I'm reopening Deveson Hall. It's been shut since my mother's death with no one to look after it but a caretaker for the grounds.'

Ravenna frowned. A stately old home like that needed constant attention and upkeep. Not just cleaning but maintenance and ongoing repairs. One of her mother's jobs as housekeeper had been to know exactly who was working where on the rambling old place.

'I'm advised it needs considerable attention.' An undercurrent of emotion coloured his words and, to her surprise, Ravenna saw him scrub his hand around the back of his neck as if to ease sudden tension. His lips pursed and she could have sworn she read concern in his features.

It was the first indication she'd seen today that Jonas Deveson was capable of feeling anything softer than bitterness or contempt.

From the way he spoke he hadn't mourned his father, yet the neglect of his family home moved him?

He was more complex than she'd thought. She'd pegged him as a man who cared for nothing but his own pride.

Ravenna opened her mouth to ask why he hadn't bothered to do something about the house earlier but the answer was obvious. He'd only just inherited the place.

Piers had spent most of the last six years out of England and hadn't visited the estate since his wife's death. Ravenna wasn't surprised to discover he'd decided to spend his money maintaining his lavish lifestyle rather than on the upkeep of a mansion he preferred not to visit.

'That's where you come in.' Jonas' slow smile chilled her anew. 'As well as the renovation work, the Hall needs to be cleaned from top to bottom. Scrubbed till it shines.'

'You want me to be part of the crew that—?'

'Not part.' He shook his head slowly, his smile growing. 'You'll be *it*. Personally responsible for getting the place ready for the ball I'm hosting to celebrate the Hall's reopening.'

Ravenna couldn't prevent herself gaping. Deveson Hall had been built centuries ago when the family employed an army of servants. It was gorgeous, precious, sprawling and the complete opposite of the low-maintenance residences being designed now. It was three floors of steady toil for the team her mother had overseen. Four floors if you counted the attics. Five with the cellars.

She had no doubt Jonas would include the cellars.

'*One person* to do all that? It's impossible!'

'There will be builders working to fix what needs repairing. You'll be responsible for getting the place ready to live in again.'

A flash of something showed in his steely eyes and

Ravenna realised he was waiting for her to refuse, to toss away what she knew instinctively would be her only option apart from prison.

'Is that all?' Somehow she choked the words out.

His smile faded.

'No. If your work is of a high enough standard then you can stay on and work off the rest of your debt as my house-keeper. That's my offer. Take it or leave it.'

The dreadful irony of it didn't escape her. Her mother might have escaped Jonas Deveson's wrath but she wouldn't. He began with putting her firmly in her place, as his servant.

Her insides twisted. She'd vowed never to be anyone's servant after seeing the way her mother had been treated by so many employers. There were wealthy employers who believed service was akin to bonded slavery. Even the sheer hard work of a commercial kitchen was preferable.

Childhood taunts echoed in her ears. Her peers had viewed sharing a classroom with a servant's daughter an insult. They'd made her pay for that insult.

Ravenna had thought she'd escaped all that.

It would take years to pay off the money. Yet she had no choice. She didn't want a criminal record or a stint in prison.

She drew a breath, trying to slow her frantic pulse.

Jonas would make her time at Deveson Hall hell, but she was strong enough to cope. He couldn't throw anything at her that was worse than what she'd already faced. She pushed her shoulders back and looked him in the eye, ignoring the sizzle of heat arcing between them.

Before she could say anything he spoke again. 'Don't get ideas of history repeating itself.' His voice was glacial. 'I don't have a weakness for the hired help like my father.'

Her chin went up. With every word he degraded what her mother and Piers had shared.

'That's a relief.' Ravenna forced the words through numb lips. 'You're not my type.'

His stony face tightened. Yet he said nothing as he waited

for her to reject his preposterous scheme. Then he'd call in the police.

'How could I refuse such a generous offer? You've got yourself a housekeeper, Mr Deveson.'

CHAPTER FIVE

THE BLEAK WEATHER did nothing to brighten Ravenna's mood. Deveson Hall was as imposing as she recalled, sprawling across what seemed acres, its blind eyes reflecting no light on this dreary, damp day.

Ravenna shuddered and wrapped her arms around herself as the drizzle-laden wind tugged her coat.

She wasn't afraid of hard work but this… She swallowed, her throat dry as the enormity of it sank in. He expected the impossible.

No sane man could expect one person to care for all that. Even if the Hall hadn't been neglected for years it needed a team of staff. He couldn't seriously think—

Of course he didn't. Jonas Deveson was no fool. He expected her to throw up her hands and surrender. He wanted to watch her admit defeat before he subjected her to the humiliation of the justice system. He'd shred her of her self-respect and rub her nose in the fact she was at his mercy.

She shuddered at the memory of his merciless gaze.

Again the furtive temptation to run sneaked into her brain. But that would solve nothing. The money had been stolen and if she didn't accept the consequences Mamma would. She was in no condition to do that. Besides, it was Ravenna who'd benefited.

She sent up a prayer of thanks that her mother was in Italy. Face to face Silvia would have known Ravenna lied when she said all was well, explaining she'd left Paris for a promising job in England.

Mamma had been so excited for her, seeing this as a chance to get her interrupted career back on track. She probably thought Jonas with his billions wouldn't miss the money. If she guessed Ravenna had accepted her guilt…it didn't bear thinking about. Ravenna felt sick to the stomach lying in their regular phone calls but she had no choice. She wouldn't leave her mother to Jonas Deveson's mercy.

Reluctantly Ravenna delved ice-cold fingers into her pocket and dragged out the key. Picking up her bag, she stepped through the weeds and up to the back door.

On the step was a carton of supplies. She ignored it as she dealt with the lock and the keypad of the state-of-the-art security system that matched the new high-security perimeter boundary.

There might be no one at the Hall but there was a full-time presence at the gatehouse security centre.

She'd been warned not to try leaving the estate lest she set off an alarm. The implication being that she was a prisoner. The shiver scudding through her turned into a full-blown shudder as she recalled the curious blaze in Jonas Deveson's pewter-hard eyes.

'Prisoner' sounded Dickensian, but that was what she was.

There would be a camera trained on this door now, eyes monitoring the entrances. Apart from keeping the place safe from intruders, Jonas probably suspected her of trying to steal the antique silver.

Was that his game? To tempt her into another theft so he'd be absolutely certain she'd get a prison sentence as a repeat offender? It seemed likely.

She grabbed her bag and entered, eager for privacy.

The flagstone hall was so gloomy she flicked on the light. The place was drear and freezing, far different from her memories. The rest of the Hall had been off limits but she'd been allowed free access to the back of the house.

She made her way to the suite of rooms Mamma had used. Rooms Ravenna had called home during summer holidays. For a weak moment she let herself wish her mother were here. She could do with her trademark optimism and determination.

Ravenna pushed open the door and slammed to a stop.

The smell hit her. A pungent aroma of damp and mouse and something rotting. Her nose wrinkled as she stared at what had once been a cosy sitting room. A breeze eddied and she turned, seeing the half-closed curtains stir as air funnelled through a broken pane.

The caretaker employed by Piers hadn't done much of a job if he'd missed something so obvious.

But the damp wasn't just from rain soaking through the hole. It streaked the walls from the ceiling. The wallpaper had green-brown smears no scrubbing could clean.

Putting down her case, she stepped forward. Debris crackled underfoot as she headed for the bedroom. The smell was worse there and the stained walls too.

Steadfastly ignoring the sound of tiny, scurrying feet, Ravenna headed back to the corridor.

Had Jonas realised the damage was this bad? No wonder he'd looked smug as he offered her this chance.

The place didn't need a cleaner. It needed ripping down and starting again! Except in a heritage-listed building things weren't so simple.

It would be a nightmare to restore, she decided as she opened door after door and found similar damage. She guessed a water pipe had burst upstairs or a drain had become blocked and these rooms had borne the brunt of the damage.

It was criminal that it had been neglected. How could Piers have been so irresponsible?

She thought of the laughing, garrulous man she'd known. He'd loved Mamma as she'd loved him. Ravenna had seen it in his eyes and in his readiness to please her mother.

But she'd also seen his self-indulgence. The way he changed the subject whenever anything unpleasant cropped up. He preferred gaiety and good times to responsibility. He'd had the look of a man who'd indulged himself for decades and he'd been a connoisseur of fine food and wine—one of the reasons he'd approved her career choice.

He'd lived a life of casual luxury. According to Mamma there was only one thing he'd been firm about and that was in having nothing to do with his family or the entailed estate he'd left behind in England.

No wonder there'd been murder in Jonas Deveson's face when he'd talked of the work that needed doing here.

Finally she came to the kitchen and hope kindled. In the grey light from the grimy windows it looked neglected rather than damaged. Ravenna released a breath she hadn't known she was holding.

At least this room was habitable. She cast a professional eye over the outdated range and badly laid out cupboards. She'd worked with worse.

The trip had exhausted her. The enormity of what faced her made her want to curl into a ball and hide.

But Ravenna had learned that the worst had to be faced. Ignoring bad news didn't make it go away.

Imagine Jonas Deveson's delight if she gave up before she'd begun! Squaring her shoulders, she turned and went to get the box of supplies.

'What's the meaning of these?' Jonas let the pile of bills flutter onto his PA's desk.

Unflappable as ever, Stephen turned from his computer. 'You said anything to do with Ms Ruggiero or Deveson Hall should come straight to you.'

'But this?' He poked a finger at the top invoice. 'Glazing?' He stirred the pile. 'Boiler repairs? Why are they coming here?'

He should have known she'd find a way to niggle at him, reminding him of her presence even though she was out of London. She should be busy scrubbing the Hall from top to bottom, too exhausted to do more than worry if he might change his mind and hand her to the police. Instead she had the temerity to interrupt him at work.

Jonas shoved aside the fact that she'd been interrupting him ever since Paris. Too often he relived the cinnamon-scented sweetness of her skin and the arousing sound of her sighs as he tasted her.

The tightness in his belly exacerbated his anger.

'Explain!'

Stephen looked at him in surprise and Jonas realised he'd raised his voice. He never raised his voice. Ever. His calm was renowned.

The only exception had been in Paris. With Ravenna Ruggiero.

He palmed the back of his neck, massaging tight muscles. What was it about her that made him lose it?

Before he could apologise Stephen spoke. 'The building project manager has been held up in Singapore. He can't start yet. I sent you a memo about it two days ago.'

He had, and Jonas, wanting only the best on the delicate job of restoring his family home, had preferred to wait a little longer to get the best in the business.

'But this?' He picked up another bill. 'Twenty mouse traps? What on earth is she doing?'

'Fighting a plague?' Stephen grinned.

Jonas rifled through the invoices again. He'd thought he could leave her to stew in her own juices for a while. But without anyone to supervise her… 'Clear my diary from tomorrow. I'm going to Deveson Hall.'

* * *

Jonas stood at the bottom of the wide front steps, a curious, hollow sensation in the pit of his stomach.

It yawned wider as his gaze crossed the weeds choking the gravel and sprouting in the litter edging the stone steps. An ornamental urn leaned drunkenly near the front door and a couple of window panes were haphazardly boarded with rough planks and even, if he wasn't mistaken, cardboard.

The emptiness in his belly became an ache and then a hard churning that riveted him to the spot. His nape prickled and something snaked through him. A searing hot sensation that wound tight around his vital organs, squeezing mercilessly till the force of it threatened to poleaxe him.

Emotions, turbulent and powerful, rose in a potent, poisonous brew.

Six years since he'd been here.

Six years since his mother took her life and his father—

Jonas clamped a lid on those thoughts, horrified at what he felt.

For six years his life had been satisfying, productive, with challenges, triumphs and pleasures. There'd been no place for emotions in his ordered, busy world.

He didn't waste time on regrets or any other pointless feelings that might distract him from his purpose. Instead he'd focused on moving forward, taking the company to even greater success.

He dragged in a slow, sustaining breath.

That was better. He had himself in hand now.

But that moment of sickening weakness, of horrible vulnerability disturbed him.

For six years there'd been nothing like it. Nothing to shake him to the core of his being. Not until Ravenna Ruggiero. Her theft, her brazen guilt, the conflicting mix of sensations she'd aroused, had unsettled him.

She was to blame.

It was as if she'd opened the sluice gates on a dam of emotion he'd walled up long ago.

He didn't like it one bit.

Another reason to have his revenge and be done with her. Surely now, seeing the magnitude of the task facing her, she'd admit defeat. There would be no more flashing eyes, no sassy comebacks, no dredging up unwanted responses.

Jonas firmed his lips and strode up the stairs.

The past hit him in a rush as he opened the massive door. A sense of long-forgotten familiarity, of childish memories and days gone by.

Of homecoming.

His hand tightened on the old wood as he fought back emotion.

There was nothing welcoming about the dimly lit room. Frigid air misted his breath as he surveyed the vast, lifeless space. Jonas absorbed the scent of dust and old wood, his gaze raking the darkened recesses, as if expecting the spectres of his past to rise up before him.

With a huff of self-disgust he strode to a window and yanked back the wooden shutters. Light spilled across the worn flagstones to the foot of the massive staircase. Overhead the shadowy beams of the high vaulted ceiling were just discernible.

Another few paces and another window, and another. Till the great hall, once the heart of the house, was revealed in its grimy glory. No sign anyone had been here in years. It looked soulless despite the faded tapestries and ancient furniture.

Jonas flung open the doors into a drawing room. More modern than the Hall, this had a fine Regency fireplace, decorative plasterwork and a massive mirror that reflected the wraith-like forms of furniture concealed beneath dustcovers.

Temper rising, he yanked open more shutters and curtains. Daylight revealed no evidence of recent habitation. His hands were grimy from the dust everywhere.

Damn it! Was she even on the premises?

He strode from room to room, letting doors slam wide to reveal neglected spaces of damp, dusty decay.

By the time he'd stalked back to the great hall that strange, unsettling feeling was gone. Instead anger burned bright and hard.

Anger against the woman who couldn't be bothered to lift a finger even to pretend to do the job he'd held out to her as an alternative to gaol.

Anger for the greedy woman who'd stolen from him.

For the woman whose mother had stolen his father, broken up his family, such as it was, and destroyed his mother.

Like mother, like daughter. Both out for an easy life. Well, not any more!

He took the stairs two at a time. If she couldn't make an effort to work on the beautiful reception rooms he knew there was no chance she'd be below stairs.

He found her three doors along, in one of the family bedrooms.

She didn't even stir at the sound of his approach. He slammed to a halt at the foot of the four-poster bed, heart beating double time as his gaze raked her.

She lay on her side, hands tucked beneath her cheek and legs curled—looking the picture of innocence.

Suspicion surged.

Was she aware of him watching? It would be remarkable if she hadn't heard him slamming through the downstairs rooms then marching up here.

His eyes narrowed but he saw no change in her breathing, no giveaway flutter of lashes.

Slanting light traced her features, throwing delicate shadows beneath her eyes and cheekbones. Tiny frown lines marred her brow as if even in sleep something troubled her.

Probably dreaming of a way to escape justice!

Jonas' gaze dipped to her mouth, softly pink and slightly

parted as if in invitation. He remembered the sigh of her sweet breath as he caressed her, the hunger to taste more.

Jonas caught himself leaning closer, hand raised as if to gentle her awake. Jerking back, he grasped the carved bedpost, anchoring himself.

He was no gullible mark like Piers. Jonas had her measure. He knew what she was, as she'd discover to her cost.

'I said it's time to get up.' The deep voice wound its way into Ravenna's sleep-fogged brain and she snuggled into the soft pillow. Just a little longer. It felt so good to let her exhausted body relax, weightlessly floating.

'Much as I appreciate the Sleeping Beauty tableau, it's not working.' The rich voice lost its mellow timbre and turned harsh, yanking her out of her hazy dream of warmth and well-being and the delicious scent of spiced citrus. In her dream strong arms had held her tight and close. Now she was alone, her skin chilled and legs cramped.

Ravenna opened her eyes and swallowed a scream as she saw him looming above her, all but blocking the light.

'You!' It was a strangled gasp, torn from tight lungs as she struggled up, scooting back against the carved headboard.

'You were expecting someone else?' Dark eyebrows slashed down in a ferocious scowl that turned his proud face into that of an avenging angel. He didn't seem to move but she had the impression he stood closer, keeping her within reach.

Panic flared and her heart beat a tattered rhythm as she read the sizzle in those narrowed eyes. Not pewter now, but the luminous silver-grey of lightning. Ravenna remembered his fury in Paris, his lashing tongue and hard, unforgiving hands that turned gentle as they curved around her breast and stroked her nipple till she all but swooned.

Fear sliced her. It had nothing to do with the taut anger in his face and wide, masculine shoulders and everything to do with the yearning that softened her traitorous body. Liquid heat rushed to her womb as she met his gaze and felt again that juddering vibration, like an unseen explosion radiating through the air between them.

Despair filled her. She'd convinced herself it had been a one-off. Some horrible aberration, never to be repeated. She *couldn't* be attracted to him. She *wasn't!*

In a tumble of limbs Ravenna scooted to the other side of the bed and off the side.

But she'd underestimated her exhaustion. No sooner did her feet hit the floor than her knees crumpled. Only her hold on the high bed stopped her collapsing.

A split second later he was there, arms outstretched as if to support her.

If she'd needed anything to galvanise her failing strength that was it.

'Don't touch me!' It came out high and breathless, choked with emotion.

Instantly he reared back, his mouth a thin line and eyes unreadable.

Dragging in a rough breath, Ravenna braced herself and stood straight. She had herself in hand now. Her legs shook like jelly but that was to be expected after the hours she'd been on her feet. It had nothing to do with Jonas Deveson.

'What are you doing here?'

His eyebrows arched high. 'I think that question is my prerogative. What are you doing sleeping *here* of all places? And in the middle of the day?'

Ravenna glanced at her watch. Two o'clock. No wonder she felt wobbly. She'd only lain down fifteen minutes ago, desperate for a restorative nap.

Since arriving she'd forced herself to her limits, ignoring earlier advice about taking things easy and allowing her body time to recuperate.

Terror was a fine motivator, allowing her to push beyond the boundaries of exhaustion day after day, knowing Jonas

Deveson would leap at that chance to accuse her of not being up to the impossible job he'd set.

And here he was. Just as she'd feared.

Ravenna swiped suddenly clammy palms down the worn denim of her jeans, vowing not to let him best her.

'I started early this morning so I was having a short… break.'

'Most people take a break over a cup of tea and a biscuit, not stretched out on a valuable antique bed.'

He was accusing her of damaging the furnishings? She might not be some delicate, petite woman, but she was hardly a heavyweight, especially after her recent illness.

Her gaze swept the bed. It was huge enough to sleep four and she'd barely wrinkled the coverlet. The rich, embroidered coverlet she'd carefully cleaned along with the full-length curtains that just a week ago had been caked in dust.

'If you're waiting for me to tug my forelock you can give up now.' She stuck her hands on her hips in a confrontational pose she hoped hid the way her legs shook. 'If I'm good enough to clean the damned thing, I'm good enough to sleep in it.'

His features tightened. 'Spoken like your mother's daughter. She must have had the same view of Piers' bed whenever she *serviced*…his room here.'

Ravenna felt the blood drain from her face at his crude implication. That Mamma was some greedy tart, using sex to her advantage.

'You b—'

'Now, now.' His voice was maddeningly superior as he raised his hand. 'Don't say anything you'll regret.'

'Believe me,' she bit out between quick breaths, 'I wouldn't regret it.' But the warning hit the mark. She couldn't afford to get him even further off side. It was only at his whim that she wasn't in police custody.

Ravenna drew a shaky breath as the surge of adrenalin dissipated, leaving her feeling ridiculously fragile. 'But since you have such archaic views on class differences, I should warn you that this is my bedroom.'

That shocked him.

Swiftly she surveyed the room she'd so painstakingly brought back to mint condition, from its plaster-decorated ceiling to its delicately shaded carpet. Old wood gleamed after multiple applications of beeswax, the soft furnishings had been painstakingly cleaned and even the crystal drops in the overhead light had been polished till they shone. He hadn't even spared it a glance.

For some reason that galled her almost as much as his high and mighty attitude.

'The housekeeper's accommodation wasn't good enough for you?' His eyes glinted a warning she refused to heed.

'The housekeeper's accommodation wasn't weatherproof or dry.' She watched shock freeze his face and knew an unholy pleasure that she'd punctured his self-satisfaction. Then her mind processed a little further, realisation dawning. 'You didn't know, did you?' Ravenna stared at his still face. 'How long since you've been here?'

Predictably he ignored her question.

'If this is your room then we'll go elsewhere for our discussion.'

It was on the tip of Ravenna's tongue to riposte with some barbed retort when she realised the sense of his words. The last thing she needed was to imprint the memory of him here, in her personal space. As it was the sight of him looming over her in the bed would haunt her for too long.

Abruptly she spun around to lead the way out. But she'd reckoned without her lingering physical weakness. Her limbs still felt like wet noodles, wobbly and uncoordinated, and for one horrible, slow-motion moment she felt herself sway dangerously and begin to topple, her arms flailing.

He grabbed her elbows, his long fingers hard and hot through the wool of her ancient cardigan.

Ravenna stared at the charcoal knit of his cashmere pullover mere centimetres away, rising and falling with each breath. Her nostrils twitched as his scent reached her, the tang of lemon and hot male skin that conjured images of long, powerful limbs, naked in warm Mediterranean sunlight.

A shudder ripped through her and she closed her eyes in denial. *No, no, no.* She was weak from what her body had been through recently, but she wasn't weak for him.

She'd have to be sick in the head to desire *him*.

'Are you all right?' No mistaking the reluctance in his voice. If he'd had time to think rather than act on instinct he'd probably have let her drop to the floor.

Slowly Ravenna lifted her gaze, past the strong contours of his jaw, up to his grim mouth, bracketed now with disapproving grooves that somehow emphasised the leashed passion in those surprisingly soft lips. She remembered the tender way they'd caressed her neck and shivered as that betraying heat swirled and swooped low in her belly again, settling and spreading at the core of her.

A tingling started up between her legs. An edgy sensation that made her want to snuggle up against him and—

'I'm fine.' Her voice was hoarse and she ducked her head rather than meet his scrutiny. Instead she felt it graze the contours of her face.

How she wished she still had her long hair. She could use it as a shield, obscuring herself from his sharp eyes.

Ravenna shook her head. Of all the things to regret, the loss of her hair was the least of them.

She stepped back, moving carefully, giving her body time to adjust. His hands dropped away instantly, as if he was only too eager to let her go.

Ravenna told herself that was a good thing. If he realised the power his physical presence had over her, he'd be sure to use it to his advantage.

They were on the landing when she spoke again. 'You haven't told me why you're here.'

'To check up on you, of course.' The words came from too close behind her. She imagined his warm breath on the back of her neck and hurried down the stairs.

'In case I was stripping the place of valuables?'

'I'm sure security would put a stop to that.' His tone was complacent. 'No, I decided you needed supervision and from what I've seen I was right.' Familiar disapproval coloured his voice. 'That's why I've decided to stay.'

Ravenna clutched the banister as the world reeled.

She'd thought this nightmare couldn't get any worse. How naïve she'd been!

CHAPTER SIX

JONAS SCANNED THE large kitchen. Old-fashioned and functional, it held a homely warmth he hadn't expected to find when Ravenna had led him to the servants' domain.

Bright sunlight revealed a huge, scrubbed table, old-fashioned wooden cabinets and a collection of brass moulds and pots hanging on one white wall. It looked like something out of the past.

His past.

He remembered having cocoa and fruitcake here, presided over by Mrs Roberts, the motherly woman who'd ruled the kitchen in his childhood. He'd often sneak in for a sample of the exotic meals she prepared for his parents' sophisticated dinner parties. She regularly patched up his scrapes and let him help roll out pastry or stir a pudding.

Until his mother had found out and put a stop to it, insisting he had more valuable things to do with his time than hobnob with servants.

Jonas blinked and turned his head, ignoring the sharp, twisting sensation deep inside and the metallic tang on his tongue. He catalogued the scrupulously clean room, the vase of evergreens on the old Welsh dresser and the way Ravenna bustled around the vast space, with an economy of movement that told him she was at home here.

The housekeeper's daughter.

She'd flung that in his face, hadn't she?

But she was far more than that.

Jonas ran a hand through his hair, watching her loose-fitting jeans pull tight and tempting as she bent to get something out of a cupboard.

His pulse thudded into overdrive as he watched her supple body. Gone was the vulnerability he'd seen earlier in her startled dark gold gaze and her clumsy movements.

Her weakness had worried him. She'd almost collapsed and it had been no act. He'd felt the tremors race through her. He'd seen the frustration in her not-quite veiled eyes and watched her work to hold herself upright, moving as if each step was an effort.

He didn't want to feel sorry for her. He didn't want to desire her either! But he'd done both. Every time he came within sight of her his hormones roared into life.

Whatever the problem it was gone now. She moved gracefully, snaring his gaze so he couldn't look away.

Jonas scrubbed his hand over his face and round his neck, massaging the stiffness from his muscles. Fat chance it would erase the stiffness elsewhere!

This wasn't supposed to happen. Not for her.

'Here.' A cup and saucer appeared on the wood before him with a plate of biscuits. Shortbread, perfectly formed and, if he wasn't mistaken, home-made.

'You're feeding me? Should I check for poison?'

She didn't answer, merely settled at the far end of the table and sipped from a cup that matched his own.

Blue and white willow pattern. It had been Mrs Roberts' favourite, brought out whenever he visited.

A jagged splinter sheared off from the twisting screw in his belly and jabbed hard.

Reacting blindly, he reached for a biscuit. It dissolved in his mouth, pure buttery comfort, like those special treats he'd devoured here long ago when his parents' blistering arguments had driven him to seek refuge in the warm kitchen.

A roaring rush of ancient memory sprang to life. Ruthlessly Jonas blanked it out.

'What's the plan? To distract me with your culinary skills?' He sounded boorish, but the alternative, letting the murky past swamp him, wasn't an option.

She didn't even look fazed, though her jaw tightened as if keeping tight rein on her temper.

That only fuelled his anger. Jonas didn't like feeling in the wrong. It was a new and unsettling experience for a man who ruled his world with confidence and authority.

'I thought for once we could have a civilised conversation. Clearly I was mistaken.' She drew a breath that lifted her breasts. Jonas' hands curled, a reflex to the memory of touching her there.

'Come on.' She shoved her chair back. 'Let's get this over with. You're dying to inspect what I've haven't done, aren't you?'

She was right. He'd stormed down here, intent on putting her firmly in her place—under his heel. Yet since arriving he'd been on edge, feeling curiously *full,* as if he barely kept a lid on emotions he'd long pushed aside. His brain teemed with unwanted memories.

Venting his spleen on Ravenna Ruggiero was the perfect antidote to those disturbing feelings.

Except now, following as she marched through the house, flinging open doors on room after room of criminal neglect, he couldn't do it.

He'd read the building report but still hadn't imagined how severe the damage was. It cut him like a blade to the heart. Anger and self-recrimination scored deep.

He'd refused to visit while Piers was an absentee landlord. He'd told himself the Hall wasn't home. Home was London, New York or Tokyo, wherever there was money to be made. He'd avoided the past and concentrated on building Devesons into the country's premier investment company.

Later, receiving the building report, he'd chosen to stay

away till refurbishment started. There'd been no reason for his personal presence.

His mouth twisted. It had been easier to stay away than remember those last months when his mother had been in such despair. He'd almost hated the place then and all it represented. Their failure of a family. His father's betrayal. His mother's depression. His inadequacy. Nothing he did or said could make things better.

He'd failed her. He hadn't been able to save her.

'Well?' The word yanked him into the present. Sherry-gold eyes sparked at him in the gloom of the damp cellar. 'Aren't you going to accuse me of slacking because I haven't fixed this yet?'

Jonas cast a cursory look over the puddles, the evidence of recent flooding, the bulging wall, and knew the sooner he got his building expert on the premises, the better.

He turned back to see her braced for confrontation. The light in her eyes challenged him to do his worst.

'It will take a team of experts to deal with this. There's nothing you can do.'

His response was utterly reasonable yet Ravenna looked stunned. More than stunned, she looked suspiciously annoyed, as if, despite her earlier words, she'd *wanted* another confrontation.

His gaze bored into hers, trying to read her thoughts, and a flush climbed her cheeks. Abruptly she looked away, lashes dropping, hiding her expressive eyes. She looked... discomfited.

Could it be that she too found it easier to trade barbed insults? And if that was a defence mechanism, what was she hiding from?

'Okay. You've shown me the worst, now show me what you've done. Or did it take all your time to clean up the kitchen and bedroom?' Given the state of the other rooms he wouldn't be surprised.

Ravenna's jaw sagged, her mouth gaping as if she'd never seen him before.

Finally he'd stemmed her flow of snarky comments. He'd fantasised about doing just that. But in his imaginings he'd silenced her with his lips fused to hers, his tongue in her mouth, finishing what he'd started in Paris.

The image erupted out of nowhere, of her melting into him as incendiary sparks ignited their bodies. It was so vivid his hands twitched, ready to reach for her. Heat drenched him despite the cellar's chill and blood roared in his ears.

His response was so sudden, so profound, it made a mockery of all the reasons he'd told himself he'd never touch her again. Upstairs, holding her steady lest she fall, Jonas had been abundantly aware of Ravenna Ruggiero as a woman. Not a thief or a parasite. Not kin to the woman who'd destroyed his mother. But as desirable.

Even in faded jeans and an oversized cardigan, Ravenna fascinated him in a way he didn't understand. He liked his women sophisticated and ultra feminine. Ravenna was feminine all right, but with a sharp tongue and prickly attitude that should have been a turn-off.

Instead—

'All right.' She spun away, turning the movement into a flounce of disapproval. 'This way.'

He got under her skin.

At least he wasn't the only one.

By the time they finished the tour Ravenna didn't know what to think. Reading Jonas Deveson when he was in a temper was easy. But now she hadn't a clue what he thought.

'*You* did that?' There'd been surprise in his voice when she showed him how she'd boarded up the windows as best she could, and the new panes the glazier had begun installing.

Did he really think she'd ignore the damage as if it didn't

matter? Deveson Hall was a beautiful old place. It deserved
better than what Piers had dealt it.

She'd shown Jonas the attic bedrooms she'd cleared and
scrubbed, with some notion of starting at the top and working down. But the rest of the vast attics had defeated her,
filled as they were with what looked like several hundred
years' accumulation of family memorabilia.

Instead of berating her for giving up on the top floor he'd
merely nodded and gestured for her to move on.

She'd shown him the gallery where she'd spent the morning on a ladder, carefully cleaning ornate picture frames,
aware all the time of rows of haughty Devesons looking
down their superb noses at her as if outraged anyone so
lowly should dare enter their presence.

Now they surveyed the bedrooms. Only one other than
hers was finished, where they stood now.

'You've done a good job.'

Again he'd robbed her of speech. Praise? From Jonas
Deveson?

Ravenna swung round to find him watching her. She
should be used to it—that piercing regard so sharp it could
scrape off skin. Or carve a needy hollow deep inside.

She blinked and tried to tear her eyes away.

'It's come up well,' she agreed. 'But I'm surprised you
admit it.' What was he up to?

He shrugged. 'It's the truth. Besides, if we're going to
be here together, I'd rather not have you glaring daggers at
me all the time.'

'This isn't about the way *I*—'

'See what I mean?' He was frustratingly superior, as if
the thickened atmosphere between them were down to *her!*

'There's no need for you to stay.' The words shot out.
'You've seen what you came to see. You know I'm not trash-
ing the place.'

'No,' he mused, frowning, 'you're not. You're actually
making a difference.'

Ravenna's hands clamped her hips. 'No need to sound surprised!'

Again that shrug. It emphasised the broad planes of his shoulders and chest and the way he blocked the doorway, making the spacious room seem too small.

'In the circumstances—' he stepped towards her '—I can be excused for doubting that. You gave the impression of a woman who's never worked in her life.'

Ravenna shuffled back, away from that keen gaze. She walked a knife edge with the truth. If she revealed too much about herself she might inadvertently let the truth slip—that it was Mamma who'd stolen his money.

'I have hidden depths.' She stopped abruptly as her legs came up against the edge of the bed. Something dark and untamed skittered through her belly at the feeling he'd trapped her there.

He paced closer, a dangerous light in his eyes. Ravenna gulped down rising tension and told herself he wasn't interested in her. That…caress in Paris had been simply him illustrating how vulnerable she was.

He stood so close she saw the beginning of dark stubble on his jaw. She remembered the soft scrape of it against her skin and sucked in a breath warm with the scent of his skin.

Flurries of sensation raced across her flesh as she met grey eyes that now looked anything but cold.

'I'll enjoy sleeping here.'

He moved and she stiffened, but instead of touching her he reached out and prodded the mattress. 'A nice, big bed,' he murmured approvingly. As easily as that Ravenna could think of nothing but how it would feel to have that long, strong body flush against hers, naked on the king-sized bed.

'You can't sleep here!' It was too close to hers, connected by a bathroom.

One ebony eyebrow arched and to her amazement she saw amusement in his face. It turned his strong aristocratic

features into something potently seductive. 'It's either that
or in your bed, Ravenna.'

'I didn't mean...'

He straightened and she sucked in a breath as the distance
widened between them. 'Forget it, Ravenna. I'm staying.
The place can't be left like this.'

Not in *her* untrustworthy hands. That was the implication. In the circumstances she could hardly blame him, yet
his prejudice rankled.

'But you've got a business to run.'

Steely eyes pinioned her. 'You really are desperate for
me to leave, aren't you?'

Ravenna tilted her chin. She was sick of lying. 'You can't
be surprised. You're hardly pleasant company.'

Instead of glowering as expected, Jonas flummoxed
her by laughing. It was a deep, rich sound that eddied and
swirled around her like a liquid embrace. Ravenna shivered and rubbed her arms, scared of how much she liked it.

'That's rich coming from the woman who thieved from
me.'

Ravenna flinched. She couldn't help it. And she regretted
it instantly, when Jonas' eyes narrowed on her face. What
did he see there? How much did he guess?

'I propose a truce,' he murmured. 'We'll behave like civilised people while we're under the same roof. Agreed?'

What other option was there? Her nerves were shredded
after an hour with him. She'd be a gibbering wreck if he
chose to prolong the animosity.

Ravenna nodded but she pretended not to notice his outstretched hand. Touching Jonas Deveson again was right up
there on her list of never-to-do experiences, like swimming
with sharks and sleeping on a bed of nails.

Two hours later Ravenna emerged into the high street of the
nearby market town, arms full of provisions. Jonas had in-

sisted he accompany her since her meagre supplies wouldn't cater for them both.

He's making sure you don't do a runner, a sour voice inside her head insisted. After all, once off the estate there was nothing to stop her disappearing except fear of what he'd do when he caught her again.

A little shiver raced through her. For Jonas *would* find her if she ran. She couldn't imagine him failing at anything he wanted. And he wanted her under his thumb.

He walked beside her, carrying the bulk of the shopping. But it wasn't his role as gaoler that unsettled her so much as his physical presence. Big, bold and aggressively male, his testosterone-charged presence challenged her in ways she didn't like to examine.

He'd been as good as his word—a perfect gentleman during their outing yet that only unbalanced her more. She could cope with his temper, even his disapproval. But there was something ridiculously intimate about the simple act of shopping together, having him insist on carrying the heavy items and even opening doors for her.

Realising how much she liked it made her edgy.

Her eyes lit on the dark red Aston Martin across the street, magnet for a bunch of admiring boys.

'You've got a very showy car.' Conveniently she ignored the fact that she adored its sleek lines and the delicious sense of being cocooned in comfort as they'd driven here.

'You think I should drive something that blends in?' Infuriatingly she heard laughter in his voice. 'A discreet dark Bentley or a battered Land Rover?' He strode towards the car. 'I worked hard for everything I've got, and I'm not ashamed of enjoying it.'

Ravenna huffed as she hurried after him, stopping as he opened the boot and unloaded his purchases. 'You were born with a silver spoon in your mouth. I hardly think—'

He turned and his expression clogged the words in her throat. She almost heard ice crackle at the look he shot her.

'Frankly, I don't care what you think.' He reached for her packages and stowed them with the rest of the food, then closed the boot. 'But for the record, I may have been born with a silver spoon in my mouth but the rest of the family silver was hocked. Piers only married my mother for the much-needed money she brought the failing family coffers. With his spectacularly unsuccessful investments and his skill at spending that disappeared soon enough.'

He leaned towards her. 'Do you know *why* I got a reputation as a *wunderkind* investor?' His breath was hot on her face but she couldn't step away. She was mesmerised by what she saw in those remarkable eyes—passion and, if she wasn't mistaken, pain.

'It was because by the time I was finishing school there was no money left. If I wanted to go to university I had to fund myself.' He shook his head. 'Hell, if I wanted to keep a roof over my mother's head I had to fund that too, since your precious Piers was incapable of doing it.'

'He wasn't my Piers.' The words came out automatically, Ravenna's mind whirling. All these years she'd imagined the Devesons living in easy luxury.

'No.' Jonas invaded her space, head thrust forward. 'He was your mother's. Did she know it was my hard-earned money she lived off all these years? Or didn't she give a damn?'

'Yours?'

His laugh had a razor edge. 'Devesons may have started as a family company but the most Piers did was act as front man. He loved that—preening publicly at our success. At *my* success. Not that he'd admit that. Easier for him to talk of the company's spectacular profits than admit it was his teenage son taking the risks and doing the work.'

'I'm sorry. I didn't know.'

With the knowledge something shifted subtly, like a kaleidoscope on the turn, pieces sliding and settling in an almost familiar yet totally different pattern. It revealed Jonas in a new light.

He'd been the breadwinner all those years, keeping Deveson Hall running and funding his parents' lifestyle? Jonas had striven to accumulate the fortune that supported Piers and her mamma?

What had it been like carrying that weight of responsibility and expectation so young?

Ravenna's teenage problems paled by comparison.

Jonas lifted his shoulders, the movement shrugging away everything but the pair of them, standing close. 'No, you didn't, did you?' he mused. 'How could you know?'

His breath ruffled her hair and suddenly his grey eyes looked soft as mist. Ravenna felt herself heat from the inside as warm treacle spilled and swirled deep in her belly. That skittering sensation was back, drawing her flesh tight.

A whirring sound intruded and Ravenna turned, startled to find a massive lens trained on them.

'Who's the girl, Jonas?'

For a startled moment Ravenna thought it must be a friend asking. But the man with the camera was backing away, camera still trained on them, as if aware of Jonas' big body tensing.

Jonas' hand encircled her arm, drawing her abruptly away and into the car.

'Damned paparazzi,' he muttered under his breath.

'Paparazzi?' Ravenna stared at the man, now two car lengths away. 'Why would they want a photo of us?'

Jonas shrugged. 'Slow news day.' Reading her frown, he added, 'Don't worry. The photo probably won't get used. And if it is—' again that wide shrug '—it's hardly damaging.'

He closed her door and got into the driver seat, apparently unfazed by the press intrusion. Which left Ravenna pondering what it was like to be so influential that even a shopping expedition was newsworthy.

They really were from completely different worlds.

It was imperative Ravenna remember that. Especially as there was unfinished business between her and Jonas Deveson, and she sensed it wasn't all to do with stolen money.

It was easier sharing a house with Jonas than Ravenna had believed possible. They avoided each other.

Yet she was hyper-sensitive to his presence. The rich murmur of his voice through a half-closed door as he spoke on the phone. The spicy scent of damp male skin that clung to the bathroom, evoking heady images of what that solid, athletic body might look like naked.

She found herself cataloguing facts about him. He made his own bed—because he was neat or because he didn't like the intimacy of her touching his bed? His weakness for shortbread and fruitcake. His habit of leaving half-empty coffee mugs about when work distracted him.

Jonas worked ridiculously long hours, running his business from a distance in between a continuous schedule of meetings with conservation officials, builders and others.

Occasionally a young man with a thin, intelligent face and a ready smile arrived, with laptop and briefcase, and the pair closeted themselves for hours. Ravenna took pity on the assistant, Stephen, and supplied refreshments. Jonas never noticed but Stephen would grin and thank her. Ravenna told herself she was glad Jonas never looked up.

She didn't want his notice. She wanted—

A betraying twist of sensation between her legs reminded her of what she'd wanted from Jonas in her dreams last night. What she'd *demanded,* and what he'd so willingly supplied.

Heat suffused her and Ravenna made herself concentrate on the next stack of leather-bound books to be lifted from the shelves.

So she had a libido. She should be glad. It meant her poor battered body was getting back to normal after the long stint of treatment.

She just wished her libido hadn't fixed on the man who'd made it his mission to wreck her life!

Ravenna laid the books on the desk and wiped her brow. It really was warm in here. She'd filled the study with every heater she could find, laying open damp-damaged books to air. But the number of books needing attention was enormous.

If only Jonas would get in staff to help her. She hadn't suggested it again, preferring to avoid him. But that hadn't worked. He was in her head all the time.

Grimacing, she yanked off her pullover. She'd worn extra layers since Jonas arrived as if they would somehow protect her. Ridiculous since he kept to himself. She could work in her underwear and he'd be none the wiser.

Grinning at the thought, Ravenna climbed the library ladder to finish clearing the top shelf.

'Careful up there!' Jonas' deep voice sounded from below, furring her arms and nape with what felt far too much like anticipation. 'I don't want you injuring yourself.'

'Afraid I'll sue for damages?' Gripping the rail, Ravenna turned. Her insides tightened at the picture he made, legs apart and arms folded, hair rumpled.

She'd thought him formidable in bespoke Italian tailoring. In a casual white shirt and faded jeans that clung to heavy thighs, he looked like a pirate. He hadn't shaved and the shadow on his sculpted jaw gave him a dangerous air. Or maybe it was the glitter in his silver gaze.

Sensation scudded through her. Something she preferred not to name. It made her feel hot and achy, needy.

She narrowed her eyes. 'Or afraid I'll squash you if I fall?' She was one of the tallest women she knew.

His mouth quirked in a sexy curl that did devastating things to her. His voice was a deep purr. 'I'm sure I'm up to your weight, Ravenna.'

He moved into the room, his gaze raking from her bare feet, cotton trousers and T-shirt to her flaming face.

She clamped her mouth shut but it didn't stop the shimmer of awareness charging the atmosphere.

'What have you got here?' He stopped by the table and picked up a small volume. Instantly the feeling of pressure in her lungs eased and she drew a slow breath.

'Those were in the small writing desk by the window. And the bigger ones are from up here.'

Jonas stood stiffly as if braced, head bent to the pages of the small book. Colour leached from his face, leaving it starkly pale, skin stretched taut over strong bones. He was so still he didn't seem to breathe. Then the pages began to flutter in his suddenly unsteady hand.

Alarm knifed her. 'Jonas?'

He didn't even look up.

By the time she climbed down he was slumped in a chair and his face was a sickly, greenish hue that made her stomach clutch. He looked as if he was going to keel over.

CHAPTER SEVEN

JONAS WAS STARING.

Ogling was probably a better word, since he couldn't tear his gaze from Ravenna's slender body. With her arms raised, reaching for an upper shelf, her white T-shirt moulded to her breasts. Her enticing, braless breasts.

Damn. He planted his feet wider, needing to ground himself, assert control over his wayward, yearning body.

He'd avoided her all week, telling himself his fascination with her would fade.

That had been a spectacular miscalculation. Every time she entered a room he lost his train of thought. He found himself staring blankly at the computer screen while she traded banter with Stephen, and his PA, still inexperienced in the ways of women, lapped up the attention.

Jonas' mouth set grimly and he yanked his gaze away, turning to the giant desk in the centre of the room. Anything other than Ravenna's distracting body.

'What have you got here?' He grabbed the first book he saw, opening it at random.

As the pages came in focus the world eclipsed.

His skin tightened. A curious ripple raced down his spine as he recognised the handwriting and the import of the words at the top of the page.

He hadn't known she'd kept a diary.

His mother had never struck him as the sort to pen her

thoughts. In later years she'd found solace and company in alcohol. But then—his gaze flicked to the date—this was an old book. Almost as old as him.

His gaze fixed on the line that had caught his eye.

Now I know it's true. Piers is having an affair.

How can he when I love him so?

Jonas couldn't help but read on, scanning the pages where the young woman who'd been his mother had poured out her despair at finding Piers with another woman. A woman who was vivacious, beautiful and confident. All the things Jennifer Deveson felt she lacked.

Jonas' stomach churned. So early in the marriage? He'd thought at least there'd been a honeymoon period. But as he read he realised Piers had had no compunction about pretending affection once the knot that bound him to his wife's money was tied.

Bile soured Jonas' tongue as he read, unable to stop. A pattern emerged. Of Piers seeking out the most gorgeous women and flaunting them. Of his wife retreating into her shell, only emerging to row with her faithless spouse.

Memories rushed back. Scenes he'd witnessed and pretended to forget. The raised voices, the threats, the undercurrent of despair. Despair so profound his mother hadn't wanted to live once Piers left her for good. What sort of sick love was that, clinging on even when it was rejected?

He'd been conceived in such a relationship?

His gut wrenched. His one dream had always been the same. To turn Deveson Hall into what it had never been in his time—a true family home. He'd fantasised about family, a real family, all his life. One that cared and shared and gathered together to celebrate the important things in life. The things his family never did.

Since he was a kid he'd imagined the Hall filled with laughter and companionship. Filled with the family he'd never had but had vowed to acquire. The gorgeous, supportive wife, the brood of happy kids. A generous-hearted matron like Mrs Roberts presiding over the kitchen. A muddle of pets, like the ones he'd never been allowed, to complete the picture.

His lips stretched mirthlessly. His imagination was as corny as a greeting card ad. Yet wasn't that why he was here? Overseeing the refurbishment ready to marry and start that family? Piers' death had been a wake-up call.

Tradition was important to Jonas in a way it could never be to a child who'd known love. He'd absorbed the legends of the house and the Devesons with an enthusiasm honed by his determination to escape the emptiness of real life. He needed heirs to fill that vacuum and share those traditions.

Now, reading his mother's despair, he felt again the helpless emptiness of his childhood.

He hadn't been important enough for her then. Nor had he been able to save her at the end.

Who was he fooling, thinking he could achieve the impossible and create a genuine family? That he could rise above the past that had moulded him? With his family history he was a foreigner to the softer things in life like love and caring. The truth smashed his long-held illusions.

'Jonas?' A hand touched his and he realised the book had fallen from his hold. He watched slim fingers mesh with his. Hers felt warm, roughened by work, but supple and capable. Feminine. She smelt of cinnamon and honey, mouth-watering. 'Are you all right?'

He opened his mouth but no sound emerged.

What could he say? That Jonas Deveson, the man who ran a multibillion-dollar business, whose views were canvassed by investors and leaders worldwide, who lived a life envied by many, was a hollow shell?

There'd been such *pain* in his mother's words. It pierced him in a place that even after all this time was raw and vulnerable.

Guilt swamped him. He hadn't been able to make things

right for her. For all his skill and corporate savvy, he'd never been good at that. He'd failed her.

'Jonas!'

His head whipped up and he saw Ravenna's concern.

He must look as bad as he felt if *she* worried about him!

Her touch was gentle as she hunkered before him. He swallowed, feeling something unravel within. Some of the tightness binding his chest slackened.

'What's wrong?' She leaned closer and he lost himself in the dark gold glow of her eyes. He focused on that rather than the darkness within.

'Nothing.' His tongue was thick and his speech slurred. 'Just an old book.'

'It's obviously upset you.' She looked down as if to reach for it and he snapped his hands around her wrists.

'Leave it. It's just history.' He couldn't believe his reaction—how long-buried emotions had rushed to engulf him as if he were some callow youth.

'I've never seen a history book affect someone like that. You look…ill.'

He felt it. Though the swirling nausea had abated a little with her touch. His hold tightened.

'I really think—'

'No!' He yanked her close, bringing her to her knees before him so she couldn't delve for the book.

'It's my mother's diary.' The words shot out, harsh and uncompromising. 'About Piers' first extra-marital affair. And the next. And so on.' He paused, listening to his blood hammer in his ears. 'Not a book I'd recommend.' He tried for casual but his voice betrayed him, emerging gruff and uneven.

Her eyes widened. 'I see.' And she did, damn her. She read him as easily as he'd read those pages for there was more than sympathy in her eyes now. There was pity.

Pity for *him!*

Everything in Jonas revolted at the idea. He'd spent a

lifetime taking on the world and winning, proving himself stronger, better, triumphant. His name was synonymous with success. He didn't need her pity.

Fury sparked, rising in a searing, seething flood.

There she was, kneeling between his legs, her expression solemn, her lips soft and desirable, the perfume of her skin tantalising and her nipples dark smudges of promise budding against her thin T-shirt. Anticipation was so strong he could almost taste her.

Lust swooped, tightening his groin, urging his legs in hard to trap her where she knelt. He welcomed it, a distraction from emotion.

This he could handle. *This* he welcomed.

Ravenna froze, her expression morphing into disbelief.

'I think I'd better get up.' Her voice was husky.

'I thought you wanted to make me feel better.' He leaned close, meeting those huge sherry-gold eyes.

He didn't want her looking at him like that, as if she could read his secrets.

'I don't think that's possible.'

'Oh, but it is.' Triumph coloured his voice as he cupped her jaw and felt her pulse hammer. Yes! That was what he wanted. Not pity or sympathy. He'd settle for something simpler and far more satisfying. And when they were done he'd feel whole again. Not like some pathetic, wounded...victim.

He slipped his hand round the back of her neck and tugged her to him, planting his mouth on hers before she could speak. And there it was, that raw spiral of heated need, spinning between them, dragging them under.

Her lips were soft as he'd known they'd be. Yet despite a week of anticipation he wasn't prepared for the delicate taste of her. Delicious. Addictive. Perfect.

Using both hands, he pulled her close, locking his thighs against her hips, imagining how it would be with her legs wrapped around his waist.

Heat shot through him and his groin was in agony, constricted by too-tight denim.

He needed her. Now.

Ravenna's head spun as Jonas dragged her into his arms with a ruthless economy of movement that spoke of practice. If she'd been in any doubt about his experience with women, his fierce certainty abolished it.

He knew women. The graze of his hard palm over her budding nipple told her that.

Yet nothing could hide his uneven breathing, or erase the pain she'd read in his face. It was his pain that had lured her close, casting aside caution.

But it was something else that kept her here. Not the taut clench of his thighs that stoked delicious awareness of his masculine strength. Nor the arm wrapped possessively around her back.

Despite the overwhelming sense of Jonas' superior size and power, despite the implacable hunger she'd read in his face as he plastered his mouth over hers, Ravenna had no fear he'd force her. Instinct, and the knowledge she'd gleaned of his pride and self-possession, told her she was safe. *If she wanted to be.*

Her mind whirled as her body responded to his urgent demands.

The truth struck her like a flare of lightning, illuminating what she'd tried to hide.

She didn't want safety. Not with his mouth reducing her to willing compliance, his body flush against hers and that heady rush of arousal in her veins. It didn't matter that they were enemies.

Maybe her response was an outlet for pent up emotions that had weighed on her too long.

Maybe she needed this rush of life-affirming pleasure after coming so close to death mere months before. She felt so *alive* in his arms.

Or perhaps she simply responded to the sheer wanton thrill of being desired by such a man: devastatingly attractive and potently charismatic, if you forgot that cutting tongue.

Right now his tongue was doing things that turned Ravenna's bones to butter.

She clawed at his shirt, relishing the taut, hot muscle beneath, and kissed him back. He tasted like last night's erotic dreams: spicy, delicious and unique. No matter how she worked she'd never create a dish with such a wonderful flavour.

Large hands slid below the drawstring of her trousers, beneath her panties to splay over her buttocks and brand her with his searing touch. He tugged and Ravenna found herself plastered against a solid ridge of denim and rampant male.

For a dizzying moment caution vied with pleasure. But her need was too strong. She thrust her hands through his hair, tugging glossy dark locks then clamping hard on his skull as she ground her hips against his.

Fire shot through her veins and the world juddered.

'Again.' The word was a hoarse rasp in her ear.

Ravenna obliged. How could she not, when the stranger who'd taken possession of her body craved Jonas as if her life depended on it?

Again she tilted her hips. They came together in a move that would have left her impaled on him but for their clothes. Light burst in the darkness of her closed eyes and she shivered at the myriad sensations bombarding her. His body, his touch, the clean smell of aroused male, even the friction of their clothes was erotic.

Ravenna tugged at his shirt buttons, whimpering with frustration when she couldn't get her fingers to work. She needed her skin against his.

'Yes, touch me.' Did she hear the words or just taste them in her mouth?

His shirt disappeared, ripped by strong hands, leaving her free to palm his torso. Blindly she traced the contours of Jonas' chest, the broad weight of hair-fuzzed pectorals, the smoother planes and ridges lower down.

She'd just reached a barrier of taut denim when abrupt movement widened her eyes. She was falling. No, not falling—Jonas' strong arm was at her back, cushioning her as she landed on the floor.

She lay on the rich antique rug as Jonas ripped open the drawstring at her waist and tugged her trousers and under-wear down.

A surge of indignant anger would have given her the strength to slap his face and cover herself. But it wasn't anger she felt.

It was excitement.

Her breath came in raw gasps as she watched him wrestle the clothes off her feet and toss them aside. His eyes glowed pure silver, almost molten, and his gaze, raking her from top to toe, was incendiary. Rivers of fire ignited in her blood, searing through anything like caution.

The way he looked at her, as if there were no one and nothing else in the world, as if he'd die if he didn't possess her…she revelled in it. For she felt the same.

She traced his powerful frame with possessive eyes, re-joicing in the heavy rise and fall of his chest and the pulse hammering out of control at his throat.

'Jonas.' His name was an aphrodisiac on her tongue. 'Come here.' She reached out and he planted a brief, fervent kiss on her palm then turned aside.

Ravenna opened her mouth to protest then realised he was tearing open a small packet he'd grabbed from his wallet. Undoing his jeans with the other hand, he moved swiftly, economically. A glimpse of his erection made her inner muscles tighten in a mix of anticipation and doubt. She was tall but—

The weight of his half-naked body on hers obliterated any doubts. He was big, his bare torso burning up, and she revelled in the way he imprisoned her, propped on his elbows to protect her from his weight.

He lowered his head, suckling her nipple through her T-shirt and she arched high, a moan of pleasure throbbing in her throat. The movement produced friction lower, where he waited at the juncture of her thighs, and lower still where her calves slid against the jeans he still wore.

Ravenna clutched his head, holding him to her breast. 'Please.' It was all she could manage, words failing her. She wanted his mouth on her but she wanted far more. She needed—

He must have understood for with one quick movement he centred himself and thrust hard and fast, right to the core of her. It was shockingly perfect, the feel of them joined so completely. For a trembling moment Ravenna felt she hung suspended from the stars, quivering in awe.

Then one large hand pushed her T-shirt up and cupped her breast. Jonas sucked on her other breast, hard and insistent, as he withdrew then surged in again, higher this time.

As easily as that she shattered. Not in delicate ripples of delight but in a cataclysmic upheaval that made her buck and scream beneath him, hands clinging and voice hoarse as she rode out a storm of pleasure so exquisite, so intense, it must change her for ever.

She was floating in ecstasy when he said her name in a voice so deep it rumbled through her, right to her bones.

Eyes snapping open, she was snared by Jonas' hot, silver gaze. In her confused state she wondered if she'd wear the brand of that intense look for life. She felt it like a touch, heavy and erotic, strong enough to mark her.

His face was austere, pared to bone and taut flesh. Then he moved, short, sharp thrusts that sent shock waves through her, re-igniting desire though it should be impossible now. It was his look that held her captive, that intense connection, the throb and push of his body in perfect sync with hers, the raw pleasure and something more, something huge and full of emotion.

Ravenna slid her hands around his hot, damp torso and down, clamping hard on the taut muscle of his backside, pulling him in, needing to share.

'Ravenna!' His voice was a roar, his eyes shocked as he bucked hard, pulsing frantically and she shattered again. This time she wasn't alone. They rode the whirlwind together, gazes enmeshed. His ecstasy was hers. Every throb and quake of delight was shared. Every gasp and groan. Every delicious shudder and squeeze of loosening muscle.

Still he held her gaze and Ravenna held him close. She reached up to those wide shoulders, tugging.

'I'm heavy.' His voice wasn't the clipped, sure one she knew. It burred soft enough to make what was left of her insides melt.

'I know.' She tugged again. 'Come here.'

He let her pull him down so they lay chest to chest, his heart pounding against hers. It felt so right, as if she'd waited all her life for this.

She'd known a man before. Just one. He'd been attractive, fun, nice. Yet she hadn't experienced anything like this feeling of completion with him. As if all was right with the world and at long last she'd found her place in it, not an outsider any more. It was as if with Jonas she was home.

Ravenna took a shallow breath, inhaling the musky scent of sex and the sharp tang of Jonas' flesh. She was barely aware of the trickle of tears down her cheek as she hugged him close.

Ravenna was limp in his arms as he carried her upstairs.

For a tall woman she didn't weigh much. There was a delicacy about her that tugged at him, made him want to keep her close.

His stride lengthened as he marched to his bedroom. Still she didn't stir. The cynical side of him wanted to assert she was playing him, trying to stir protectiveness. But he'd seen her stunned expression as she'd climaxed not once, but twice. He'd felt her convulse around him in great waves of pleasure that shook him to the core.

Jonas had never experienced anything so intense. It was as if her passion had turned him molten and forged him into someone new. He felt…different.

His arms tightened. Was it like this with her every time?

He'd known Ravenna was passionate. Her vibrancy, whether in fury or indignation, had fascinated from the first, drawing him despite himself. If he'd known how that translated to erotic passion he'd have followed through on that kiss in Paris instead of waiting all this time.

Satisfaction stirred as he nudged open the bedroom door. *This* was what he wanted from her. Sex. The sort of passion that drove out anything as corrosive as pity. He didn't need her feeling sorry for him. He was no charity case.

Jonas laid her on the bed, taking in the beguiling curve of her full lips and those lustrous, long dark lashes that fanned her rosy cheeks. Something unfamiliar skated through him as he looked down at her. Tenderness. The need to look after her.

The realisation slammed into him, catching his breath. Already his hand had reached out as if to trace Ravenna's cheekbone, the pure angle of her jaw, the delicate pulse at her throat. His heart skipped a beat as he remembered the look in her eyes as they'd climaxed together. The wonderment and joy. A joy so strong it had branded him.

Jonas snatched his hand back.

Even asleep Ravenna was dangerous.

He assured himself this wasn't different from what he'd experienced with other lovers. It *couldn't* be different. If he felt altered it was only because of the depth of his arousal. He couldn't remember ever needing any woman with such a primitive urgency.

Jonas nodded, satisfied with that explanation. He knew

what he wanted from Ravenna and it wasn't emotion. He'd never felt emotionally bound to a lover and he wasn't about to start with her of all women.

When the time came for feelings they would be for his wife. The perfect woman who would fit his requirements and his world, who'd excel at being a mother, a gracious hostess, a social success and a loyal, supportive spouse.

Jonas frowned. For the first time his vision of the perfect wife to create his perfect future didn't fill him with anticipation.

He looked at Ravenna, noting the graze of stubble rash on her cheek where his unshaved jaw had rubbed and how the damp patch on her T-shirt clung to her nipple where his tongue had laved.

He felt a primitive satisfaction that he'd marked her as his.

His chest tightened and a frisson of doubt snaked through him. No! This was lust pure and simple. Not to be confused with his longer-term plans. Those plans had been all that kept him sane in a world where no one cared for him except as a pawn in the game of his parents' disintegrating marriage or, later, as the goose that lay the golden eggs. His family, his women—all had only wanted what he could give them. They hadn't wanted *him*.

So he'd learned to take.

He let his gaze rove Ravenna's slim legs, bare and supple, to the V of dark hair between her thighs. His sex stirred, eager for more.

That was what he wanted. Physical pleasure and release. He could seduce her awake or have her again while she slept. But he did neither.

His gaze caught on a red mark on her hipbone. It was where he'd gripped her hard as he came. White-hot memory of that glorious cataclysm rocked him. And more, of the soft light in her eyes when she'd tugged him to her and wrapped him close in trembling arms. She'd had nothing to gain from that embrace. It had been about giving, sharing,

and he couldn't remember anything better than those moments in her arms, not even that spectacular orgasm.

Silently Jonas shucked off his jeans and climbed onto the
wide bed, careful not to disturb Ravenna. The bed shifted
beneath his weight and she rolled towards him. Automatically he put his arm around her, tugging her close, her head
on his shoulder, her hand at his hip. His breath snared at the
innocently erotic pleasure of her touch but he made no move
to wake her. For now this was enough.

He wrapped his other hand around her thigh, dragging it
over his belly, and sank back into the mattress.

It seemed hours later that she woke. Her lashes tickled
his chest as they fluttered open. Her fingers twitched as if
testing the surface she lay on. Instead of rearing back in
horror she nuzzled closer as if drawing in his scent. All his
senses went ballistic.

She blinked sleepily up at him, her lips widening in a
smile that knocked a chunk of granite off the corner of his
heart. Her gaze was warm and for the first time he saw her
smile reach her eyes. They glowed.

Jonas felt something shift deep inside. Something he had
no name for. He felt it again when her hand skimmed up and
around and he found himself being cuddled.

Hugs weren't common in his experience, even after sex.
He discovered he liked them. They made him feel…good.

Who'd have thought 'good' could be so satisfying?

'Thank you.' Her voice was low, shivering through him
like a caress.

Another first. How many lovers thanked him even though
he put their pleasure first?

Guilt pummelled him. He hadn't been careful with
Ravenna. He'd taken her with a savagery that bordered on
uncontrolled. Look at the way he'd bruised her.

'Are you okay?'

She blinked at his rough tone and moved as if to prop

herself up to see him better, but he kept her clamped to him. He liked her right where she was.

'Okay? I feel fantastic.' Her smile turned secretive and her lashes lowered as her cheeks coloured.

A woman who blushed and thanked him for taking her with the finesse of a horny teenager? Ravenna was far from the woman he'd imagined.

'I didn't hurt you?'

She shook her head. 'I told you I enjoyed it. Didn't you?' Ravenna's voice was like warm whisky spilling through his veins and pooling low in his belly. She looked him square in the eyes and Jonas' heart give a great thump.

'Absolutely.' *Enjoy* didn't come close to describing what he'd felt. 'But I should have been more careful. I've bruised you.' His hand drifted to her hip, caressing the spot where he'd held her.

Her lashes dipped, hiding her eyes as she shrugged. 'I bruise easily. But it doesn't hurt.'

'Good.' Jonas told himself he should end this, get up and walk away. But he couldn't. His fingers feathered the soft skin at her hip and he heard her hiss of indrawn breath.

'In that case,' he murmured, slamming a door on the voice of caution crying out in his head, 'perhaps we might do it again.' He watched her eyes widen with anticipation and felt satisfaction flare. Satisfaction at the thought of having Ravenna again, of taking his time to pleasure her slowly. Of sharing that oneness again.

'I never thought I'd say this, but you have some good ideas, Jonas Deveson.' Her smile was sexy as she trailed a finger up his throat to his ear.

Arousal jolted through him. Swiftly he rolled her onto her back, capturing her wrists and dragging them above her head. At her moue of disappointment, he leaned in and tasted her mouth, shocked yet pleased to discover her as delicious as before.

'Let me, Ravenna. I want to do this slowly.' He feathered

tiny kisses down her neck, then moved down and licked the underside of her breast, unbearably turned on just by the taste of her and by her uneven breathing.

'I'm not sure I can bear it.' But the look in her eyes belied her words. It was warm like a caress as it locked with his. Again he felt that unfamiliar clenching in his chest.

In that moment it was far more than sex that he wanted.

CHAPTER EIGHT

RAVENNA WOKE IN Jonas' bed. Smiling, she rolled on her side, reaching for him. He wasn't there.

Her stomach dipped. She'd never imagined herself insatiable but an afternoon with Jonas had taught her things she'd never expected.

That she had erogenous zones she'd never known.

That she could make Jonas lose his cool.

That ecstasy made her noisy. Her face flamed at the way she'd screamed his name over and over. But he hadn't minded, encouraging her as if he enjoyed hearing her shout his name.

That she had a weakness for silvery eyes, a broad chest and clever hands that knew exactly how to touch her.

That she had a weakness for Jonas Deveson.

Her breathing quickened. Jonas wasn't the frigid enemy she'd thought. He had his own difficult past. He'd been the one supporting his family and her mother, from the day he left school. Was it any wonder he'd had no time for Piers or Silvia, who'd kept their distance yet lived off his hard work?

As for his mother… Ravenna bit her lip, remembering his wretchedness as he read that diary. Whatever else Jonas might be, he wasn't unfeeling. He'd been raw with pain. It had hurt to see him so.

When he'd made love to her it hadn't been a cheap little wham, bam, thank you ma'am, no matter how fast and furious the first time. She'd felt so much. They had shared more than mere physical coupling. And his tenderness here in his bed—

Ravenna wriggled under the sheets. The next time he'd been gentle, utterly devastating with those careful caresses, until the white-hot urgency overtook them again.

It had been wonderful, far beyond her imaginings.

The explosion of passion had been inevitable. She'd been too inexperienced to understand the frisson of sexual tension from the moment he'd stalked into the Paris apartment. All she'd known was that around Jonas she was on edge, as if her skin didn't fit. She'd put it down to hatred, not attraction.

Ravenna watched the door. Jonas would be back soon. Their relationship had changed irrevocably and they needed to work out where they went from here.

It wasn't so much sex that had changed their relationship, but the sense of intimacy. She knew him for a more complex, feeling man than she'd imagined. And he knew she was more than the grasping thief he'd believed, or he wouldn't have let her get so close. He was too proud to open himself to a woman he disdained. The knowledge buoyed her.

Tantalisingly, Ravenna felt on the brink of understanding Jonas. Not completely, but she realised his original antipathy came from the harsh realities he'd faced. She'd seen a hint of the scars he'd carried since childhood.

In that moment she despised Piers. He'd been good to Silvia and she was grateful, but to ignore his own son…!

Whatever difficulties Ravenna and her mother faced, they'd had each other. She couldn't imagine growing up so alone. Jonas hadn't spoken much of his relationship with his mother but she guessed it hadn't been easy. What she knew of Piers' wife made her seem self-focused rather than maternal.

A shiver passed through Ravenna. She and Jonas still had a long way to go. The money was an almost insuperable barrier. Ravenna couldn't simply blurt out the truth.

Jonas detested her mother and would love a chance to make her suffer if he learned it was she who'd stolen from him.

But surely now Ravenna could make him listen and he'd be more understanding. Things weren't black and white any more. Behind the lord-of-the-world façade was a man she wanted to know better.

Given time they'd work things out. It wouldn't be easy, or immediate, but eventually he'd understand.

Through the bathroom door her mobile phone rang. The insistent ringing grated, high pitched like nails clawing her sensitised skin. Maybe because she'd faced such bad news in the last year she couldn't ignore it—had to check it wasn't something important.

Scurrying to her room, she snatched up the phone and draped a rug around herself, chilled after leaving Jonas' bed.

'Ravenna?'

'Mamma? What is it? Are you all right?' Her stomach curdled at Silvia's tone. They'd spoken only yesterday. What had happened since to put the fear in her mother's voice?

'I'm fine. It's you I'm worried about. What has that man done to you?'

Ravenna stilled in the act of shrugging the rug closer.

'What man?'

'Oh, *Ravenna!*' It was a wail of horror. 'So it's true. I can hear it in your voice.'

'What's true? What are you talking about?' It was impossible Mamma had guessed she was with Jonas. Yet, standing naked, aching in unfamiliar places after his thorough loving, Ravenna felt as if she'd been caught out.

'Don't pretend, darling. I know you're with Jonas Deveson.'

Ravenna sank onto the bed. What on earth was going on?

'I saw it in a magazine. You and him shopping together.'

'A magazine?' It must have been the paparazzi shot that had so surprised her.

'The press have labelled you his secret girlfriend. They

say the pair of you are holing up in a love nest.' Her voice rose in panic. 'Tell me it's not true. Tell me you wouldn't be stupid enough to fall for him.'

Ravenna opened her mouth then shut it again. Everything was moving too fast. She felt dizzy.

'Ravenna?' Her voice was sharp. 'Has he hurt you?'

'Of course he hasn't hurt me, Mamma. You're overreacting. There's nothing to worry about.'

'Nothing to worry about?' She could almost see her mother roll her eyes. 'You're such an innocent when it comes to men. There's nothing innocent about the way he's looking at you in that photo. He looks like he wants to eat you all up.'

Heat scorched Ravenna from her toes to the tips of her ears. That was precisely what Jonas had done, using his mouth on her body to reduce her to quivering desperation.

'Ravenna.' Her mother's voice, now quiet, vibrated with worry. 'Tell me you didn't fall for his lies.'

'Jonas isn't a liar, Mamma.'

'Oh, Ravenna! You did, didn't you?'

Ravenna squared her shoulders. 'I'm twenty-four, Mamma, not a little girl. Jonas hasn't hurt me.' Given her mother's response to that innocent photo, now wasn't the time to reveal the whole truth. Her mother would hotfoot it to England and that would set the cat among the pigeons. Much as Ravenna wanted to see her, Silvia was safer in Italy. 'I'm…working for him, as a temporary housekeeper.'

'That's the job you were excited about?' Silvia was disbelieving. 'You vowed never to work in service.'

It was true. Ravenna had determined never to be anyone's servant after years of being made to feel inferior at school.

But that was before her mother had stolen and put her in a situation where she had to swallow her pride. Mamma had taken the money for *her*. This was her responsibility.

'Jonas is hosting a ball to reopen the Hall and I'm doing the catering. It will be a great opportunity to showcase my skills.' Ravenna was babbling but couldn't stop. Maybe because she was naked, her body tingling from his touch. 'I hope it will be a stepping stone to other jobs.'

Her mother sighed. 'Promise me you'll keep your distance. He hates me and he'd do anything to hurt me. You have no idea how ruthless he is—' her voice dropped '—or how much he despises me. He blames me for his mother's death. But I swear I had no idea she still cared about Piers. While I was at the Hall all she did was snipe at him. Poor Piers—'

'I know.' Ravenna had heard it before, how Piers had fallen in love for the first time ever with her mamma. How happy they'd been. 'But Jonas can't hurt me.'

He already had his retribution. What more could he do?

'Don't be too sure. Even when he was young he had a way with women, a magnetism that drew them even though it was obvious they were expendable.'

Ravenna bit her tongue rather than snap that if he had, he'd probably got that from his father. Her mother hated hearing anything negative about Piers. He was one of the few subjects they didn't see eye to eye on.

'I wouldn't put it past him to seduce you, just to settle the score. He's charismatic and persuasive but beneath the charm he's cold and calculating.'

'Maybe there's more to him than you think. Besides, it was Piers, not Jonas, who ripped that family apart.'

Silence greeted her words. It was the closest she'd come to criticising Piers to her mother. He'd been good to Silvia and he'd loved her in his own way, but she'd never been comfortable with his irresponsible take on life.

'I know.' Her mother's misery caught at Ravenna's heart.

'I'm sorry, Mamma. I—'

'No, don't apologise. It's just I'm worried about you. No matter what you think you know about Jonas Deveson, remember this: he's an aristocrat through and through. He's not easy-going like his father. He's a perfectionist who only settles for the best. To him that means a woman from the right family, with the right connections, the right accent, the right look. You'll never be that woman. To him you'll always be the housekeeper's daughter. Worse, you're a permanent reminder of me and Piers.'

A weight crushed Ravenna's chest as she heard her mother say all the things she'd told herself. But that was before—

'You'll find the right man one day, Ravenna. But it won't be Jonas Deveson. At best he'd offer a brief affair. At worst—well, you only have to look into his eyes to understand the meaning of revenge.'

Ravenna swallowed. She'd seen that look. That day in Paris it had transfixed her with a fear she dared not show.

'I'm sorry, Mamma,' she said quickly. 'I have to go. But don't worry. I'm perfectly able to look after myself.'

So why, when she ended the call, did Ravenna feel shaken to the core? Jonas didn't love her—she wasn't that naïve. But there was something between them stronger than prejudice. Something drew them despite the reasons they shouldn't be together. It was worth exploring.

Tossing aside the rug, Ravenna went to her wardrobe. It was time she squashed those poisonous tendrils of doubt.

She reached for a pair of trousers and paused. Call it feminine pride but she wanted him to look at her with desire. Ravenna pulled out the one decent dress she'd brought.

It felt disturbingly as if she donned protective armour.

Ravenna was back in his bedroom when he returned. At the sight of her tucking in sheets with swift movements, he almost wondered if he'd imagined the last, passionate hours when they'd driven each other to ecstasy again and again.

His gaze dropped to the length of her legs, revealed as she leaned across to plump up the pillows, and the sweet curve of her bottom against the clingy orange dress.

Jonas swallowed over sandpaper as his body stirred.

Then she turned and he saw what she wore. Not the nondescript work clothes he'd fantasised about stripping off her all week. The dress was held in place by a single, provocative tie at the waist. A V neck hinted at her delicious cleavage, but it was the way the dress clung that made his heart hammer. Like lover's hands it cupped, caressed and flowed over proud breasts, the swell of her hips and a waist that he could almost span with his hands.

She was blatantly sexy. Her gaze collided with his and that white-hot blast of connection shimmered in the air.

Hunger slammed into him as if he hadn't already had his fill of her several times. Instead of sating desire, an afternoon spent in bed had turned him into a randy teenager, driven by his libido, not his brain.

It unsettled him. He ruled his world through logic and careful planning. Yet he'd lost a precious afternoon's work and all he could think of was how many moves it would take to have Ravenna naked beneath him again.

He raked his hand through his hair. He'd left her to seek refuge downstairs, needing to gather himself, yet just one look shattered him all over again.

'Jonas.' Her voice had a low, throaty quality that would make him think about sex even if she were wearing a sack. 'I was just coming to look for you.'

She approached then halted as if having second thoughts.

'I was busy downstairs.' Busy revisiting that diary. When that got too much he'd taken refuge in thoughts of Ravenna coming apart in his arms, more radiant and alive than any woman he'd known.

'Oh.' She wiped her hands down her dress, instantly dragging his gaze to her thighs and flat belly.

Jonas drew in a breath redolent with the tang of feminine arousal. He'd yanked his clothes on without bothering to shower. Till this moment he hadn't admitted it was because he revelled in the scent of her on his skin.

He frowned. Why? What made her different from other women?

He hadn't even come back here in the hope of more sex.

She'd been so exhausted he'd expected her to be asleep. He'd simply returned to be with her—she made him feel good.

That was a first. An unsettling one.

'Why did you want me?' It came out gruffly but for once Jonas was incapable of charm.

Ravenna shrugged but the movement was jerky, betraying nerves. 'I thought we should talk.'

He nodded and prowled further into the room. 'Go ahead.'

Her eyes widened before she looked down, lashes veiling her eyes. Silently Jonas cursed the loss of even the most basic courtesy. No morning after had ever been so awkward. He had a horrible suspicion it was because none had ever felt quite so important. He was ridiculously on edge.

'We need to talk about us.'

Every male instinct Jonas possessed hummed to alert.

'Yes?' He noted the way her gaze skated over his shoulder then to a spot below his ear.

'About this afternoon.'

Suddenly her uncertainty made sense. He'd been careful about protection, as always, but that last condom had torn. He hadn't realised she'd noticed and had told himself the chances of it leading to anything were slim.

'Are you on the pill?'

'No.' Her gaze jerked to his. It wasn't worry he saw in her face but something indefinable. Instinct told him it was something she didn't want him to notice.

'I see.' That complicated matters. Suppose she got pregnant? It wasn't what he'd planned, but he'd never walk away from a child of his.

The idea of Ravenna being pregnant with his seed shafted possessiveness through him. 'If there's a child—'

'There won't be a child.' Her expression was shuttered.

'It's possible.'

She shook her head and he read obstinacy in her jaw. 'You don't have to worry about it.'

His belly twisted hard. His mother's diary had revealed

with brutal clarity why he was an only child. After him there'd been an abortion and she'd ensured she didn't have another baby to the man who'd betrayed her. Jonas had thought he'd plumbed the depths before, but that revelation had torn a gaping hole somewhere in the vicinity of his chest.

'Why?' The word shot like a bullet. 'Because you'd terminate it?'

Ravenna's face froze. 'No! Because I know my body and you don't have anything to worry about.'

Air escaped his tight lungs and he realised he'd been holding his breath. 'I see.'

Ridiculous to feel a pang of regret.

'So what did you want to discuss?' He stepped closer but made himself stop at arm's length.

'Us.' She waved one arm in a gesture that encompassed the bed. 'I mean, what happens now?'

Jonas could think of several things he'd like to happen. All involved Ravenna naked. He moved forward but stopped, seeing her draw herself up stiffly. He remembered how demanding he'd been. She could be sore. Jonas tried to feel guilty but couldn't bring himself to regret what they'd done.

'Things aren't the same now.' She fixed him with a keen gaze. 'Are they?'

What did she want? An admission that she'd turned him inside out with her sexuality, indomitable spirit and devastating generosity? That moment in the study when she'd offered comfort had undone him. He was so unused to anyone's concern, he'd repudiated it even as secretly he coveted it.

He hadn't managed to fathom what it was he wanted from Ravenna, except more. Until he understood he'd admit nothing.

'Jonas?' Her tone sharpened.

'What happens now?' He shrugged, not liking the sensation of being cornered. 'We both have work to do.'

Her stare grew fixed. 'Is that all?'

'No, of course that's not all. I want to take you back to

bed.' His gaze dropped to the V of her neckline. 'Hell! I don't even want to wait that long.' Heat surged in his blood and his lower body grew heavy and hard. 'But given the fact you're up and dressed I'm assuming you don't feel the same.'

Jonas enjoyed the fiery colour slashing her cheeks. It reminded him of her full body blush when he made love to her.

'I'm not talking about that.'

'No?' He jerked his brain back into gear. 'What else is there?'

Her eyes widened and he felt a moment's regret. But he refused to be railroaded into discussing *feelings,* if that was what she meant.

'I see.' Ravenna's jaw tightened and she crossed her arms. Did she realise how that plumped up her breasts? 'So as far as you're concerned we'll go on as before, except for bouts of hot sex when the fancy takes you.'

'It's an improvement on what went before.'

She didn't respond to his smile.

He wondered how long it would take to seduce her into breathless compliance. His body stirred. He'd always enjoyed a challenge and despite her frosty attitude Ravenna would welcome him. Look at the way her nipples budded and her pulse throbbed in her throat.

'Let me get this straight.' She unfolded her arms and stepped into his space, her eyes glinting gold sparks. 'After what we shared you think nothing has changed, except you get rights to my body whenever you want?' She shook her head. 'You're in the wrong century, Jonas. The droit du seigneur vanished ages ago.'

He stiffened. 'No one forced you, Ravenna.' Her sceptically raised brows grazed his pride, for he hadn't been gentle that first time. But nor had she been forced. Ravenna had made a choice. She could have refused. 'You wanted me.'

'I did,' she finally admitted. 'But that doesn't mean you can expect me to slave away here under your Draconian conditions and be your sex toy as well. You can't have it both ways. I deserve better.'

Jonas surveyed her defiant face, her pouting lips, fuller from his kisses, her reddened cheek where his stubble had marked her. Anger flashed in her eyes and something like disappointment.

His gaze dropped to the seductive flame-coloured dress designed to bring a man to his knees.

His belly curdled as finally, and far too late, realisation struck. Jonas almost staggered under the impact.

How had he been so blind? Disappointment carved a hollow through his vitals. Disappointment and fury at his naivety. Him, naïve! You'd think with his history he would have expected this. Yet he felt sick with the shock of it.

Just like her mother, Ravenna aimed to sell her body for a rich man's favours. She saw him as an easy target and wanted to buy her way out of debt. She thought sharing her body wiped out her crime.

That put what they'd done together in a new light.

Anger and resentment swamped Jonas—that he should have responded, wanted so much, when all the time it had been a tawdry transaction by a conniving woman.

Ravenna watched storm clouds gather in Jonas' eyes. That leaden stare sent a chill scudding down her spine. It was as if they were back to the animosity of Paris.

Stoically she forced down rising bile. Had she deluded herself? Had the man she'd begun to feel for been an illusion? Had his vulnerability and his easy charm been as her mother had warned—a ploy to make her lower her guard so he could wreak revenge on her family?

She didn't want to believe it.

'What did you have in mind, Ravenna?' His voice was a low purr, but instead of soothing it made her hackles rise. He sounded like a hungry lion inviting her to dine.

She lifted her chin. 'I was hoping to talk. Get to know

each other better.' The words sounded lame in the face of his cool regard but she plunged on. 'I thought we might come to a better arrangement too about the work to be done here.'

'Really?' One saturnine eyebrow rose in lofty surprise.

'Yes, really.' His condescension sliced through her caution. 'If you want this place put in order I'll need help.'

'You don't think you should dirty your delicate hands now you've slept with the boss?'

That sarcastic tone scraped her skin raw. She felt sullied, pressing a hand to her stomach as nausea rose. Familiar exhaustion struck, dragging at her limbs, making her panic she wouldn't be able to stand up to him physically.

Not now. Not in front of him!

'In case you hadn't noticed my hands aren't delicate.' They were firm and capable, bearing nicks from her apprenticeship in a commercial kitchen.

Jonas shifted, looming over her by a head, making Ravenna feel every inch of the difference between them. From his chiselled, aristocratic features to his elegant handmade clothes and designer watch he was the epitome of wealth and authority. She, with her shorn hair and cheap, chain-store dress didn't fit his world. She'd never been ashamed of being poor, but she'd always hated condescension.

This was worse, far worse.

'You know what I mean,' he said, his voice low and lethal. 'You think because we had sex I'll forget your crime? Or are you setting your sights higher? Do you think I'll keep you in luxury now I've had a taste of what you're bartering?'

Ravenna rocked back at the force of his contempt.

'All I *want*,' she ground out between her teeth, 'is a little respect.'

'Is that what you call it? And there was I, thinking you were simply whoring yourself like your mother.'

Ravenna's hands clenched as she fought the urge for violence.

'You really are a self-satisfied bastard.' He didn't even flinch, whereas she felt as if she were crumbling.

'And I'm sorry to say you're every inch your mother's daughter. I warned you, I don't share my father's weakness for the hired help.' His smile killed something fragile inside. 'But that doesn't prevent me taking what's on offer.' His eyes stripped her bare and she shuddered.

'There's *nothing* on offer.' Not any more. Not when he'd taken her caring and her concern, and, yes, her body, and reduced them to nothing with a few slashing words.

'Let's get one thing straight, Ravenna.' He leaned closer, invading her space. 'If you're aiming for something permanent you're barking up the wrong tree.' His voice was rough, reminding her of the sharp emotion she'd seen in him when he talked of his family. Yet his eyes had the blank look of someone who'd shut himself off from feelings.

She wished she could do the same.

She wished her mother had been wrong and Jonas was even half the man she'd begun to believe him. Mamma had been right—Ravenna had confused sex with caring. Now she paid the price as pain sliced her.

'Don't worry. I get the picture. As far as your family is concerned the Ruggiero women are good enough to be mistresses but never wives.' From some inner reserve of strength Ravenna summoned a shaky smile. 'Frankly, a long-term relationship hadn't occurred to me. I'd like to respect the man I live with. But thanks for the clarification.'

Ignoring his glare, she turned away, careful to keep her balance on wobbly legs. When the door shut behind her it was with a snick of finality.

CHAPTER NINE

JONAS TOSSED THE design portfolio onto his desk and sat back, rubbing eyes gritty from lack of sleep. He couldn't concentrate. He hadn't been able to concentrate since that scene with Ravenna.

Ruggiero women are good enough to be mistresses but never wives.

The look on her face as she'd thrown what he was thinking straight back at him! Defiance, hauteur and a pain that cut to the bone. It was that anguish, etched in her eyes and taut frame, that had dragged him from blind fury long enough to recognise he might have overreacted.

Might have? He'd jumped down her throat without hearing her out.

Because it was easier to dismiss Ravenna as a gold-digging opportunist than believe she could be something more.

Yet it was the something more he'd responded to, not just her sexuality. It was the woman who'd comforted him, her enemy. The woman who, without being asked, catered cheerfully for those working around the Hall, even him, the man set on making her life hell. The woman who had rolled up her sleeves and taken on the ridiculously impossible task he'd set her, revealing a grit and determination he'd not thought possible. The woman who'd fought him tooth and nail but never shied from the consequences of her actions in thieving from him.

He shook his head. Something didn't add up, but he was too befuddled to work it out.

Jonas looked at his half-empty mug and the scatter of crumbs on the plate she'd left on his desk and felt remorse.

Good enough to be mistresses. The pain in her words made him feel two inches tall.

No woman deserved to think that. Especially the woman who'd shared herself so unstintingly while he'd behaved with the finesse of a Neanderthal.

In Paris he'd thought her a consummate liar, a woman totally changed from the earnest, engaging teenager he'd met. But that scene in his bedroom proved him wrong. Ravenna couldn't hide her shame and anguish as she faced him down.

He felt like scum.

As if he'd taken advantage of her.

For the first time he wondered how Ravenna had reacted to her mother's affair.

The teenage Ravenna had seemed heartbreakingly alone in a world that judged merit on status and money. She'd suffered at the hands of bullies who despised her lack of wealth. Yet she hadn't envied their money, just hated their shallowness.

How had she felt when her mother took up with Piers, revelling like a self-satisfied potentate in the furore over his gorgeous mistress? Had Ravenna enjoyed the ride?

Or, the thought struck hard, had she cringed at the gossip about her mother leeching Piers for cash?

Ravenna had developed that shell of pride for a reason.

Once the thought lodged he couldn't shake it. Especially as he recalled the wretchedness she'd tried to hide when he'd accused her of sleeping her way out of trouble.

Guilt smote him. Perhaps it was true. Perhaps not. But the memory of that haunted look discomfited him.

Jonas shoved back the chair and strode across the room.

He halted when he saw Ravenna talking with his garden designer, Adam Renshaw. The man's auburn head was bent towards hers and fire seared Jonas as if he'd been skewered on a spit. He couldn't breathe.

It took a moment to identify the unfamiliar feeling as jealousy.

His jaw tightened. He wanted to stomp out and haul Ravenna away.

As if he had a right to her.

As if she wouldn't simply ignore him after what had passed between them.

Jaw gritted, Jonas admitted that no matter what he wanted, no matter what Ravenna wanted, this wasn't over. They had unfinished business.

His mouth twisted mirthlessly as he registered something like relief at the knowledge.

The women in his life had always been expendable. Even the Honourable Helena Worthington, the blonde beauty with impeccable bloodlines and a sweet disposition whom he'd half decided on as a future bride. She hadn't been important enough to stop him taking Ravenna to bed.

Yet with Ravenna, for the first time in his life a woman seemed infuriatingly *necessary*.

He had to discover why.

Then find a way to free himself.

Jonas swung away, almost knocking over the easel of samples his interior designer had set up. His gaze slid over dark paint and patterned fabrics. He'd wanted traditional but this was… He shook his head. Too predictable?

Then he noticed the sheet of paper Ravenna had brought with his coffee. Concise bullet points listed matters needing attention. Every day she presented him with another list of problems—from damage to wainscoting to cracked tiles, usually with suggestions on how to deal with them. She had an eye for detail and a flair for organisation. Qualities that didn't sit well with his original judgement of her.

Jonas looked from the list to the design portfolio. They

were talents he could use. And they would keep her out of the garden and in here, where he wanted her.

'Sorrel, chervil, sage, fennel.' Adam Renshaw smiled. 'There must be at least three dozen herbs on this list.'

'Too many?' When he'd asked Ravenna, as interim house-keeper, for input to his garden design, enthusiasm had over-come her bitterness about Jonas.

How could she resist the opportunity to help plan what promised to be a superlative cook's garden? She daydreamed about having such a place, with space for not only herbs and vegetables but fruit trees and berries. Just walking in this garden with its mellow stone walls and gnarled apple trees lifted her spirits. Something she needed badly.

The alternative, dwelling on Jonas, was untenable.

'Not at all. It's good to have your input.' Adam moved closer. 'We'll fit them in easily over there. I just need to check the final design with Mr Deveson.'

'Did I hear my name mentioned?'

Ravenna froze as that familiar, rich voice curled around her like velvet on bare skin. Her lips compressed. How could she react that way when the same voice had lacerated her just days ago?

Adam swung round to face their boss. Ravenna took lon-ger, bracing herself before she met his gaze. Would it be coolly dismissive or would he ignore her as he'd done this morning when she'd brought coffee and he'd been absorbed in a huge portfolio?

Neither, she realised with a jolt as she turned. His gaze was as intent as ever but with none of the chill she expected. Nevertheless she moved half a step closer to Adam, aware of those dark pewter eyes narrowing.

She lifted her chin, reminding herself she didn't care what Jonas Deveson thought.

She'd been naïve to believe she could bridge the chasm between them. He'd used her and made a mockery of what she'd felt. The knowledge kept her chin high and her gaze steady.

'Of course,' Adam was saying, when she finally tuned in to the conversation. 'Ravenna and I were plotting the herb beds, but I think we've got it now.' Warm brown eyes smiled at her approvingly and she wished she could summon a spark of excitement for this pleasant, talented man.

Instead her attention focused on Jonas, standing preternaturally still, just watching the pair of them.

Her mouth flattened in self-disgust. No matter how hard she tried she couldn't ignore him.

'Excellent. In that case I'll just borrow Ravenna.' Jonas turned to her. 'If you have a few minutes?'

She raised her eyebrows. Jonas was requesting, not ordering? Suspicion rose but she forced herself to nod, bidding Adam a warmer than necessary goodbye. This was the first time Jonas had sought her out since that scene in his room and her stomach knotted. What did he want?

'You two seem to get on well,' Jonas said, holding open a door for her to enter.

'Adam is good company.' And attractive. And clearly interested. But Ravenna's pulse didn't quicken when he was around. Yet now, walking beside the man who despised her, she couldn't control her racing pulse.

'Do you have a lot in common?'

She swung around to face Jonas, livid at his feigned interest and at herself for being so weak. 'Why do you ask? You're not interested in my personal life. Only my ability to scrub floors or spread my legs.'

A flush coloured those high cheekbones. 'I deserve that.'

His admission did nothing to mollify her indignation or self-recrimination. She took a deep breath and looked away. 'What do you want, Jonas?'

She was so weary. Her chores had been almost beyond her lately as she fought an exhaustion she hadn't known for some time. At the back of her mind lingered the worry that perhaps her illness had returned. That worry gnawed at her, keeping her awake at night. That and thoughts of Jonas.

'In here.' He gestured to the open study door.

Squaring her shoulders, she entered, studiously averting her eyes from the dark carpet on the far side of the room where they'd come together in such urgent passion.

Cheeks flushed, she took a seat by the desk. If he was going to tell her he'd finally decided to call the police to deal with the theft she'd rather be sitting.

'I'm sorry.'

It was the last thing Ravenna expected. She jerked her gaze up to find Jonas standing over her, as tense as she'd ever seen him.

'I beg your pardon?'

'I said, I'm sorry.' He waved one arm in a gesture of frustration. 'I'm no good at this, but I'm trying to apologise for what I said. What I did.'

Ravenna blinked and stared. 'For what exactly?'

Jonas rubbed his jaw and she heard the faint scratch of bristles. Her skin heated as she remembered that roughness against her skin. Just looking at his unshaven jaw made her stomach tighten as erotic recollections filled her head. She shivered. Her thoughts were dangerously self-destructive.

His lips twisted ruefully and despite everything she couldn't help the little tug of attraction deep inside.

'Not for the sex. I can't regret that.' His smile disappeared. 'But for later. The way I acted, what I said about you.' He breathed so deep she watched, fascinated, as his chest expanded. 'I was crass and hurtful.'

Ravenna stared. 'You're saying you don't think I tried to buy my way out of trouble with my body?'

'I'm saying I don't know enough about you to judge.'

It wasn't what she wanted to hear but at least it was honest.

Yet did she want to wait while he took his time learning to judge her on her merits? Why should she?

Because she had no choice. She was trapped here.

More importantly, despite everything, she couldn't turn her back on Jonas.

That spark of fire between them had morphed into something that tied her to him, no matter how she tried to sever the connection. As if she still believed the half-formed hopes she'd harboured when she'd met him, passion for passion, as an equal rather than a bonded servant.

That scared her more than anything.

'I behaved badly, accusing you the way I did.' His voice was deep with regret. 'I should have listened. Especially after…' he shrugged and spread his hands in a gesture that seemed curiously helpless '…after your concern for me.'

He looked as if he were swallowing hot coals. As if he wasn't used to anyone's concern. Or being seen as vulnerable.

That realisation dried the caustic response forming on Ravenna's lips.

As her gaze meshed with his it wasn't the heat of anger or lust she saw there, or his familiar stonewalling expression. She read uncertainty in those grey depths, as if he'd lowered the shutters to let her glimpse the man behind the façade of authority. The man she'd discovered the day they'd shared passion so fierce it had burned away everything else and left her feeling raw and new.

'And so?' Ravenna forced herself not to trust the regret she thought she read in Jonas' features. Only days ago she'd been duped into believing he felt something for her.

'And so I regret what I said.'

Ravenna nodded. He watched her as if expecting a response but she said nothing. Words were easy. It was actions that counted.

'And I've decided to make some changes.'

Here it comes. Ravenna clasped damp palms together. *He's calling in the police.*

'I'm bringing in extra staff. Not just the builders but some local people to help with the cleaning and heavy work.'

Ravenna searched his face for some hint of a catch.

'But you said—'

'I know what I said. Looking after the Hall was to be your penance.' His lips compressed as his gaze swept her. 'I was unreasonable.'

Her jaw sagged as he met her eyes almost defiantly. She couldn't believe her ears.

'There's no need to stare as if I've got two heads.'

'Are you feeling all right?'

Jonas gave a bark of laughter. 'I should have known you wouldn't just say thanks. You wouldn't let me off easily.'

Let *him* off? He was the one in control. Ravenna stared, bemused, as laughter softened the grooves around Jonas' mouth and eased the severity of his austere features.

She swallowed, fighting fizzing awareness.

'And what about me? Are you pressing charges? Is that it?'

Jonas' expression sobered. 'No. Not for now. You'll stay and work as my housekeeper.'

Not for now. He still held that over her. What had she expected? That without evidence of her innocence and in the teeth of her admission of guilt he'd let her go? Impossible!

'But I'm hoping we can continue in a more…civilised way.'

Ravenna sat straighter. 'If by civilised you mean sharing a bed because I'm supposed to be grateful you've brought in staff—'

Jonas' raised hand stopped her. 'I've never had to buy my way into a woman's bed, Ravenna. I won't start now.'

Heat scored her cheeks. Once had obviously been enough for him. Once with the hired help to satisfy his curiosity.

'It's time to take some of the heat out of this situation.' He looked at her long and hard, as if attempting to read her mind. 'I'm trying to be reasonable, Ravenna. We can't continue as before.' He sighed. 'Contrary to what you might think I'm not prone to outbursts of temper.'

She did believe it. She'd learned all she could about her nemesis and there had been plenty. The consensus was that Jonas Deveson was one of Europe's most eligible bachelors, wealthy, charming and urbane. He was known for his incisive mind, impenetrable calm and careful planning. Employees and competitors respected him and his generosity was renowned. As was his drive to succeed. There was no mention anywhere of a temper or strong passions.

Which left her wondering why, with her, he'd been anything but calm and controlled.

A tremor whispered down her spine.

Perhaps it had something to do with the way her emotions undercut caution and good sense when he was around.

'So you'll treat me as your housekeeper and I'll treat you as my employer?'

After what had passed between them was it even possible? The strain of the last couple of days had almost broken her.

'That's the idea.' He nodded. 'To step back from the rest.' His wide gesture encompassed all that had gone before: the animosity, the flagrant desire and the illusion of closeness that had betrayed Ravenna into believing they shared something special.

'How can I refuse?' That was safest. No more dangerous, incendiary desire. No fireworks. She should be thanking her lucky stars, not feeling dissatisfied, as if a rug had been pulled out beneath her.

'Thank you, Ravenna.' Their eyes met and she felt a now-familiar jolt of heat. The awareness hadn't gone away.

Jonas turned away and she breathed deep, searching for equilibrium. He offered a truce and this time she was determined nothing would break it. If she had to stay here with him, it would be strictly on a boss-employee basis.

'In the circumstances I thought you might help me with this.' He turned, the large portfolio in his hands.

'What is it?'

'Come and look.' He put it on the desk.

Ravenna stared from the album to his broad back in charcoal cashmere. She didn't want to stand beside him. It was easier to maintain her poise if she kept her distance.

'Ravenna?'

Reluctantly she crossed to the desk, keeping as much distance as she could from Jonas. He turned the pages, revealing swatches of colour and design, all rich but rather ponderous and dark.

'I told my designer I wanted a traditional feel. But it's not working.'

He stopped at a page showing one of the drawing rooms. There were fabric swatches in deep, rich hues, heavily decorated, and photos of imposing antique furniture. It would be like living in a museum.

'You see what I mean?'

Ravenna straightened, realising she'd been leaning over the page, imagining the finished room and disapproving.

'Why show me? I'm just the housekeeper.'

'You know this house better than anyone, apart from me.' He picked up a sheet of paper and tossed it on top of the portfolio. Ravenna saw it was a list she'd made of repairs. 'You've got a good eye for detail and a feel for the place.'

She raised her eyebrows. 'Where are you heading, Jonas?'

'I thought you might have some thoughts on what would suit the old place.' His eyes met hers then shifted to the portfolio. Because he was up to something or ashamed of his earlier behaviour? Ravenna wished she could read him.

'I'm the housekeeper, remember? This is what you pay a designer for.'

'Most women would jump at the chance to plan a redecoration.' His tone was persuasive.

'I'm not most women.' Her hands crept to her hips. Despite his apology, his earlier accusation still rankled.

'No, you're not. Most women would have run screaming from Deveson Hall the moment they saw how much work it needed. But you didn't.' His deep voice was rich with what sounded like admiration. 'Others might have made a mere token effort at the job, but not you. You've been boarding up holes and drying out damp books on top of everything else. You make lists of repairs. You've even sourced local suppliers so work can begin quickly.'

Jonas paused. 'You've betrayed yourself, Ravenna.'

She started, horrified that somehow she'd given away her mother's secret.

'You've shown yourself to be a woman who cares and takes pride in what she does. I'd like to have you work with me. If we could set aside our differences I believe we'd deal well together.' He spread his hands in a gesture of openness. 'Of course, I'd take your assistance into account when it came to determining how long it takes to pay off your debt.'

Ravenna braced herself on the polished desk, her pulse hammering. She told herself it was relief that her mother's guilt was still secret. Or disappointment that he still held that debt over her head.

The alternative, that it was reaction to Jonas' praise, wasn't an option.

'When you put it like that, how can I refuse?' She tore her gaze away and made a show of concentrating on the samples. 'So long as you don't hold it against me if the result is a disaster. I have no decorating experience.' Furnishing her bedsit with second-hand pieces hardly counted.

'Don't worry, I'll still use the decorator. I just want another opinion on some things. Like this.' His finger jabbed a page showing the study.

Ravenna took in the handsome, heavy furnishings in the design, the deep green colour and the use of dark wood. She guessed nothing in the proposed design was less than a hundred years old. Even the light fittings were modelled on old lamps. Just looking at the page made her feel claustrophobic.

'What do you think?'

She shrugged. 'You said you wanted traditional.'

'But?'

'How honest do you want me to be?'

'I've never had a problem with honesty, Ravenna.'

She met his bright gaze and knew an almost overwhelming temptation to blurt the truth. To explain about the money and her mother's desperation. To resolve the lurking tension between them so she could be free of the burden of secrecy and Jonas' bad opinion. But love for her mamma stopped her. Ravenna couldn't leave her to his not-so-tender mercies.

'It's like something out of Dickens.' She waited, trying to read his expression. 'Or a movie set of what an old-fashioned gentleman's residence should be.'

'My feelings exactly.'

'Really?'

He nodded. 'I couldn't work in a room like that.'

'What *do* you like?' Her curiosity stirred.

Jonas waved his hand towards the long windows. 'Light. Space. A comfortable chair built to take a man's weight and a desk high enough for my knees.'

Ravenna surreptitiously scanned his big frame. She'd never thought of Jonas' height being an issue. He always looked supremely comfortable whatever his surrounds.

'So keep this desk. It's a bit battered but the wood is lovely. I'm sure an expert could restore it beautifully.'

Jonas' mouth turned up at one corner and Ravenna felt a little tug as if someone pulled a string through her insides. 'That's one decision I'd already made. The desk stays. But what about the rest?'

'What colours do you like?' She forced the words out, mesmerised by that half-smile. It evoked intimate memories she'd tried and failed to bury.

'Gold,' he murmured, his voice low as he leaned close,

looking straight into her eyes. 'Old gold, something like the colour of a good aged sherry.'

Ravenna felt his breath on her face like an elusive caress. Her skin drew taut and the tugging sensation in her abdomen became a heavy thrum. Her pulse sounded in her ears as she swayed.

Blinking, she stepped back, wary of the way his low, masculine purr resonated through her. Once bitten...

Deliberately she turned. It was ridiculous to imagine Jonas had been describing the unusual colour of her eyes.

'Tell your designer you want gold.' She surveyed the walls. 'Or maybe lighter. What about a soft straw? Something more neutral so the woodwork doesn't overpower the room?'

'That could work.' From the corner of her vision she saw him finally look away towards the walls. 'What else?'

'You said a comfortable chair. What did you have in mind? Do you mean for working at the desk or a sofa?'

'Both. I like the chesterfields.' He waved a hand at a couple of sofas that needed reconditioning. 'But there's a young German designer who does brilliant ergonomic chairs in minimalist design.' Jonas frowned. 'But would that clash?'

Ravenna read his abstracted look and realised Jonas really wanted her opinion. When he'd suggested getting her input she'd thought it some ploy. Instead he was genuine.

Something softened inside. She hoped it wasn't her defences.

He met her eyes, a hint of familiar impatience in his expression. 'Well? What do you think?'

Ravenna shook her head. 'That's for your designer to advise. How about I make a list? Can you pass me a pen and paper?'

CHAPTER TEN

RAVENNA PULLED HER jacket close and stepped out briskly. Even after a couple of months getting used to the bustle of building work, she preferred early morning solitude.

She surveyed the house, its stones mellow in the early sun, its new glazing glittering. Despite its size the Hall felt welcoming, maybe because she'd come to know it intimately. She'd delved its crannies, supervising cleaning and small repairs, and helped Jonas plot the refurbishment of what would be a marvellous home as well as historic treasure.

Turning, she crunched her way along the gravel path, wishing she could turn her mind as easily from thoughts of Jonas. His presence pervaded the place, even though he spent half the week in London. From London he rang regularly to check progress, his deep voice never failing to send a thrill of pleasure through her.

Life had fallen into an easy, if busy, routine since his apology. A routine Ravenna found a little too easy given Jonas still held her future in his hands.

Surely it wasn't right that she cared so much for a place she'd leave as soon as her debt was paid? Or enjoy Jonas' company? She laughed too often at his dry humour over the restoration's inevitable mishaps and delays.

He was patient, flexible and understanding. All the things she once thought him incapable of. Plus he appreciated her efforts, thanking her when she catered for emergency meetings with contractors and heritage officers, or when she helped him sift decorating suggestions.

She enjoyed the latter most of all. She told herself it was because she loved having input to the way the grand old house would look. It had nothing to do with the camaraderie that had developed between them as equals, rather than boss and servant.

Jonas had never come on to her again—he kept his distance. It was as if that day they'd spent exploring each other's bodies had been a dream.

Except her body remembered the pleasure he'd bestowed so lavishly. It quivered in anticipation when he approached, or when she inhaled his scent of citrus and warm male.

There were times when she'd swear she saw heat in his polished silver gaze. A heat that reflected all the things she told herself she shouldn't feel for Jonas. Since his apology the vicious, vengeful man she'd met in Paris had disappeared, replaced by one she liked far too much.

Ravenna quickened her pace, passing a drift of spring flowers, only to pause at the sounds from the newly restored stable block. Jonas had mentioned animals being delivered yesterday.

The stables had been empty while Silvia worked here and Ravenna had never seen thoroughbred horses up close. She followed the path to the nearest door.

'There now, Hector. That's better, isn't it?' Jonas' voice halted her in mid stride. 'That's my beauty.' The words were a slow thrum of approval. Obviously he was gentling some highly strung stallion, but, even knowing his words weren't for her, Ravenna felt the murmur like a caress on her skin.

Her heart dipped. Most of the time she coped with her situation, telling herself she was almost over the feelings Jonas evoked. But coming upon him suddenly, unprepared for the impact of those deep baritone cadences, her instant response told its own story.

How long before she could shake off this volatile attraction?

'Tim, you're in the way. There will be time for you in a moment.' Jonas laughed and she couldn't resist inching closer.

The sight that greeted her stopped her in her tracks.

There was Jonas in scuffed boots, worn jeans clinging to bunching muscles and a plain black T-shirt that stretched across a torso that was all hard-packed strength and perfect proportion. His dark hair was tousled and his skin glowed. He looked like a pin-up for the outdoor lifestyle.

But it wasn't just his breathtaking male appeal that sent the air scudding from her lungs. It was the joy in his expression. Unadulterated happiness that turned his strong features into something so powerfully appealing it wrapped tight fingers around her heart.

Ravenna had seen him smile, heard his wry humour, had even heard him laugh, but she'd never seen him look so happy.

And the cause of his happiness? A sway-backed draught horse that nudged him as he brushed it and a chocolate Labrador that lurched between man and horse, its tail waving.

'Watch out!' Ravenna darted forward as the horse shifted and the dog wandered into the path of its massive hoof.

Man, dog and horse all turned to stare. An instant later the hoof descended harmlessly as the dog hobbled towards her with a ruff of pleasure.

'He's only got three legs.' No wonder the dog had wobbled so badly. She dropped to her knees so it could sniff her hand then lavish a rough-tongued caress on her wrist.

'Timothy! Back here.' Jonas moved towards them. 'I'm sorry. He's a bit too enthusiastic.'

Ravenna laughed as the dog tried to lick her face. 'No, don't worry. That's fine. I like dogs.' She looked up into silver eyes and felt a jolt right to her core.

'So I see.'

Ravenna blinked, telling herself she couldn't feel Jonas' gaze. As for the way her lungs had constricted… It was as well she was booked for a medical check-up soon.

'Look out!' she warned.

But it was too late. Jonas staggered towards her after being nudged by the draught horse's massive head. He braced himself before her, legs planted wide as she looked up into his laughing face.

'Obviously Hector doesn't like his routine being interrupted.'

'Hector?'

A large square hand reached down to her. Automatically she took it, letting Jonas pull her up. For an exhilarating moment they stood toe to toe, then he let go and moved back.

'Meet Hector.' He raised a hand to the massive animal's neck and the horse whinnied as if in response.

At Ravenna's feet the lopsided Labrador looked up expectantly, tongue lolling.

'I suppose this is Timothy.' The dog barked at the sound of its name.

Bemused, she looked around the stables. The stalls were deserted but for this one.

'*These* are the animals you brought in? They're not yours?'

Jonas shook his head. 'I'm giving them temporary accommodation as a favour to a neighbour. Part of her stables burned down due to an electrical fault and she put out an SOS for Hector. Where Hector goes, so does Timothy.'

The dog hopped over to the big horse, which lowered its head and gusted its breath over the Labrador.

'That's…very nice of you.'

'But not what you expected?' He didn't miss her surprise.

She shrugged. How could she say caring for a lame dog and an old horse wasn't how she saw him spending his spare time? She hadn't known he *had* spare time.

'I thought you'd bring in thoroughbreds to ride.'

'Later. For now Hector needs a home.' He patted the horse. 'Didn't you, old fellow?'

'You know him?' There was familiarity in his tone.

Jonas nodded. 'Hector was saved from the knacker's yard when I was a kid. Vivien, my neighbour, finds homes for unwanted animals—donkeys, goats, ponies, even a three-legged dog and a blind draught horse.'

'He's blind?' Ravenna stepped closer and saw Hector's eyes were cloudy.

'Pretty much. But he's got Timothy, who leads him where he wants to go. Together they make a good team.' He ruffled the dog's ears then picked up the brush he'd been using.

'I spent a lot of time at Vivien's when I was young. She taught me to ride and help out. Hector was venerable then.' Absently Jonas rubbed the horse's neck and it struck Ravenna she'd never seen him so relaxed, except for the day they'd spent sprawled in his bed, boneless and spent from ecstasy.

Fire seared her cheeks and she bent to pat Timothy, who'd hobbled back to her. 'I'd imagined you learning to ride here.' She waved her hand around the enormous stables.

Jonas turned away to brush the big horse, but not before she saw the shutters come down, eclipsing the laughter in his eyes. 'My mother didn't ride and Piers had other things to do with his time.' Wide shoulders shrugged. 'He spent most of his time in the city and when he was here he had interests other than teaching me.'

The edge to Jonas' voice made her think instantly of comments he'd made about Piers chasing women. Not much of a father then.

'So you spent a lot of time at your neighbour's?'

'Enough to learn to ride and to care for animals.' His words were matter of fact but his tone confirmed the experience had been precious.

'Didn't you have animals here at the Hall?' She stepped closer, needing to know more.

* * *

Jonas flicked a warning look over his shoulder. He didn't welcome prurient curiosity. But the sight of her, bent to scratch Timothy behind the ears, even while she looked up at him with serious eyes, gave him pause.

'Pets weren't allowed. My mother wasn't an animal person and Piers...' Jonas shrugged. Piers had rarely been around long enough to express an opinion. As for teaching him to ride! His father had never taken time out from his own pursuits to be with him. Even on those occasions when his parents had temporarily made up, Jonas wasn't a priority.

Jonas watched Ravenna's expressive eyes flick from him to Hector. 'You like horses?'

'I don't know. I've never met one up close.'

Jonas remembered the first time he'd visited Vivien's stables, the excitement tinged with fear that had turned to delight. 'Come and meet Hector. He's very gentle.'

She hesitated for so long he thought she wouldn't come. Why it was important that she did, Jonas had no idea. But it felt good when she approached, as if she trusted his word.

'Here.' He took her hand, fishing in his pocket for one of the sugar lumps he'd brought. He dropped it onto her open palm and drew her in front of him.

Sensing a treat in store, Hector snuffled at her hand. Instantly Ravenna stepped back, her curves enticing even through her jacket.

'No, don't drop your hand.' He held hers up and flat. 'Hector won't bite.'

'He's so big.' She leaned back, her shoulders pressing into his chest, her riot of newly grown dark curls tickling his chin. She smelled of cinnamon and sugar, and beneath them was the scent of her pale skin, an unnamed but heady perfume that he greedily inhaled.

He'd missed her, missed the right to touch her. Every day was a battle not to reach for her, to palm her soft skin, taste her, draw her close and have his fill.

'Oh, you beautiful boy,' she crooned as Hector lipped up the treat then nodded as if in thanks. 'Did you see that? How he took it from my hand?'

'Mmm, hmm.' Jonas strove to suppress the arousal that fired as Ravenna whispered her delight to Hector. She wasn't even talking to Jonas yet the low thrum of her voice and the press of her body almost made him forget his promise to keep his hands off.

'Here.' He found the curry comb he'd been using and sidestepped, taking Ravenna along with him till she stood at the horse's shoulder. 'You can groom him.'

'Can I? How?'

The best way to demonstrate was to put the comb in her hand and cover it with his, moving them both in slow sweeps.

Hector shifted and Ravenna shrank back. Jonas smiled as he wrapped his other arm around her waist to hold her steady. Or perhaps it was a grimace, given the exquisite torture of holding her and not revealing his needy reaction.

'You're safe. Hector is a gentleman.' Their joined hands traced a wide arc across that broad equine shoulder and side.

'And you're here to protect me.'

Had he heard right? The indomitable Ravenna needing protection?

'Did you visit your neighbour and her animals often?'

'As much as I could. It was so *alive* there, always something happening.' He watched their hands move in tandem, telling himself he'd step away soon.

'I'd have thought the Hall would have been busy too. I seem to remember quite a few servants and tradespeople when I visited.'

Jonas dropped his hand, letting her continue alone. 'As son of the house I was kept separate from that.' And he'd hated it. 'My early memories of the Hall were of solitude. There never seemed enough people to fill it and a house like this needs people. When there were visitors it was for formal dinner parties to which small boys weren't invited.'

'You make it sound like you were on the outside, looking in.' Ravenna half turned then seemed to think better of it, leaning in to comb Hector with a long stroke that moved her backside temptingly against Jonas' groin.

He should move away, should drop the arm wrapped around her waist, before she sent him over the edge. But he couldn't shift his feet.

'Not all the time.' He didn't want her sympathy. 'The kitchen was always welcoming and then there was Vivien's and the animals.'

'It still sounds lonely.'

He watched the curry comb slow almost to a stop.

'I was no lonelier than lots of homes.' He had no intention of sharing exactly how bleak his childhood was. 'I remember you here, just behind this stable block, crying your eyes out because someone named Pamela had made your life hell at school. Because you were excluded.'

Ravenna's hand slid to her side. 'You remember *that?*' She'd never thought he'd recall in such detail.

'I remember feeling sympathy for someone else who felt like an outsider.'

Ravenna stiffened as the memory of ancient pain surfaced. He saw too much. Then it hit her he'd made it sound like something they had in common. Both outsiders.

She spun around. Jonas was so close her pulse thudded in response. She saw deep into his eyes, could even count his spiky dark eyelashes.

He was so near one tiny move would bring them together. A half-step, a tilt of her head, and they'd be kissing. The air between them crackled and heat saturated her skin. Her fingers tingled, anticipating the feel of his smooth-shaven jaw. Surely he'd moved closer?

Her breath hitched audibly and suddenly there was distance between them.

Ravenna blinked. Had she imagined that moment of intense expectation? The way their bodies swayed together?

Hurriedly she gathered her scrambled thoughts.

'But you fitted in. Your family has been here for centuries. You were born to all this. You *belonged*.' She waved her hand wide. 'I never did.'

Move back, she told herself. *It's too tempting, too dangerous. You're too close to Jonas.*

But her body wouldn't listen. She stood, looking expectantly into his dark face.

His mouth curved in a half-smile that was poignant rather than amused.

'You belonged, Ravenna. You had your mother, remember? You were close. Even now I can't help feeling that she's mixed up somehow in the reason you're here.'

Ravenna opened her mouth to protest but his raised palm stopped her. 'I'm not asking for your secrets, Ravenna,' he said, surprising her. 'I'm just saying you always had her on your side. She loves you.'

She nodded. That went without saying.

'Then you were lucky. Luckier than a lot of kids.'

Like Jonas.

'Who did you have, Jonas?' The housekeeper he'd spoken of so warmly now and then? His neighbour, Vivien? Everything he *hadn't* said about his parents confirmed what had been lacking in his family: warmth and love.

'I had myself.' Not by a flicker of an eyelid did his expression change. He looked strong, proud and sure of himself. All the things she'd seen in Paris when she'd thought him arrogant and self-opinionated.

But now Ravenna realised there was much more to him. The man who'd lost himself in her body. Who, in his grief, had needed her with a desperation that scorched through every barrier. Who now distanced himself again.

With a fervour that surprised her, Ravenna wished for a return of the intimacy they'd shared. She wanted—

This wasn't about what she wanted.

'Was that enough?' Suddenly it struck her that Jonas' sometimes superior air, his confidence, his determination to get things right, no—perfect, every time, might be traits he'd learned in his youth to overcome loneliness and doubt. Had they been defence mechanisms for a little boy desperately in need of love? Mechanisms that had become habit in the man?

His dark eyebrows rose. 'Every child wants to be at the heart of a big, loving family, don't they? But I was luckier than a lot. I had food and warmth. I had an excellent education.' His stare dared her to feel pity for him. 'And I had this—Deveson Hall. I knew one day it would be mine and then I'd make it right.'

'Right?'

'Absolutely.' His eyes shone. 'I had a lot of time to dream as a boy. I spent my days exploring the Hall, absorbing its history and traditions and planning how it would be when it was mine. The old place became my family in many ways. It was my mainstay.'

'So that's why you're here through the renovations.' Ravenna had wondered why he didn't stay in London and leave the detail to his project manager. She'd thought at first it was because he wanted to keep a close eye on her.

'I want the job done properly.'

There was that perfectionist streak again. Everything had to be done just right before Jonas would be satisfied.

'You wanted it furnished in a traditional style to match what you'd known when you were young?' Or more probably, from what he'd said, to bring it up to a standard he'd never known as a child when money had grown shorter each month.

Jonas shrugged. 'Maybe. Though my tastes have changed. Traditional with a modern twist perhaps.' He strode to the open stable door to gaze at the Hall, automatically stooping to pat an adoring Timothy, who shadowed him.

'When it's done I'll hold a ball. That's a Deveson tradition that got dropped over the years. This year it will be a turning point.' Jonas turned and she read anticipation in his face. 'I'll want you there, Ravenna.'

Her heart fluttered, till she reminded herself the housekeeper had a vital role in any big house function.

'Of course. I'll supervise the catering.'

He nodded. 'It will be a big job but we'll do it.'

Ravenna felt a tiny jolt of pleasure at his 'we'. They worked well together, perhaps because of the unspoken boundaries they'd been careful not to cross.

'But I don't want you behind the scenes.' His gaze collided with hers and her skin tingled at the approval she saw there. 'After all your hard work I want you at the party, not in the kitchen. You deserve to celebrate too.'

Ravenna blinked, a tiny trail of fire flaring in her blood. It was the closest he'd come to hinting he'd forgiven her for the money. Would the celebration signal the end of her servitude? The weight she'd borne so long lightened a little.

Working in service reinforced all the insecurities of her youth. Despite the ease of the past couple of months, it still stuck in her craw to be a servant, especially here.

'Ravenna?' Jonas watched her expectantly. 'You'll come?' So it wasn't an order. It was an invitation. Ravenna smiled.

'Of course. How could I miss celebrating you achieving your dream?'

He shook his head. 'Not quite. This place is my heritage, a part of me. But the refurbishment is just the first step.'

'Really? What else is there?' She reached up to stroke Hector's cheek as he snuffled at her pocket, searching for treats. She could get used to the warm, comfortable smell of horse and hay. In fact, she could get used to life at Deveson Hall with an ease that surprised her.

Jonas surveyed the mansion that had come to life under his supervision.

'I loved this place as a kid but even I could see it wasn't a home. It was cold and unloved, despite the best efforts of our housekeeper.' He paused so long Ravenna thought he wouldn't go on.

When he spoke again it was in a low, musing voice that made her wonder if he talked more to himself than her.

'That's what I want. A home. Something more than the apartments in London and New York. A place with heart.' He shoved his hands in his pockets and rocked back on his feet. 'A place for a family. A wife who'll love the place as I do. We'll fill the old place with children.' He bent to pat Timothy as the Labrador bumped his leg. 'And a muddle of dogs and other animals. I'll make it a real home.'

Ravenna clutched Hector's mane.

Home. A family.

It shouldn't surprise her. Why else renovate Deveson Hall? Jonas wouldn't want to live there alone.

Fill the old place with children.

Her stomach dipped in an abrupt roller-coaster curve that hollowed her insides, turning them queasy.

She'd listened to Jonas' plans for the Hall with an approving smile. Wistfully she'd almost seen herself as part of that, despite her resolve to keep her emotional distance. In a hidden chamber of her heart had lurked the hope that one day they could put the past behind them and start again—pursue that connection she still felt to him just as strongly as the day they'd shared their bodies.

Then he'd mentioned children.

Her hand crept to her cramping belly, over the womb she knew was barren.

Months ago, shocked at the news of her cancer diagnosis and the need for early action, she'd told herself infertility was a small price to pay for the treatment that would give her a chance to live.

She'd always wanted children but she was young, yet to find a man with whom she wanted to spend her life.

Ravenna had concentrated on being grateful she'd survived, refusing to regret what couldn't be cured—the chance to bear her own children.

But now the void within yawned wide and pain poured in.

She was crazy ever to have imagined she could build a relationship with Jonas. Everything stood against it. Their history. The theft. Her background and social status. She didn't fit in his world. She never would.

And she could never give any man children. She was strong, capable and worthy of a good man's love. But she lacked—

Hot tears prickled her eyes and she blinked. She hadn't cried through months of treatment. She wouldn't start now.

Quietly, leaving Jonas to his dreams, she turned and slipped out through the other door.

CHAPTER ELEVEN

JONAS MANOEUVRED THE Aston Martin through the city streets on autopilot. His attention was all for Ravenna, sitting pale and subdued beside him.

These last weeks she'd changed. They still worked well together but that spark of camaraderie, that sense of being *comfortable* together had gone.

Perhaps it was his fault for not addressing the question of how long he expected her to work for him. The money she'd taken was substantial, but the effort she'd put into Deveson Hall had been remarkable. Without her organisational skills, eye for detail and hard work there'd be no celebratory opening ball next week.

Who could blame her for wanting to end their arrangement?

Yet he'd avoided the issue. He couldn't imagine the place without her.

The realisation made him frown.

No one was indispensable in his life. No one except the wife he'd marry once the Hall was ready.

He'd spent the last couple of years considering potential brides, taking his time sorting through likely candidates before settling a few months ago on Helena Worthington. Beautiful, gracious and warm-hearted, she'd make an excellent spouse and mother. Born and bred on her family's vast country estate, she lived in London, working at an exclusive gallery. She had the skills to make him an excellent hostess.

One of the reasons for the ball was to see her in his home and check he'd made the right choice before finalising his plans. They'd been out a few times in the past and she was definitely interested, but he'd kept things light till he was sure.

Beside him Ravenna shifted. He really should talk to her about the future.

He could offer her top dollar to stay permanently as housekeeper. She'd run the Hall with the brisk efficiency and empathy for the place that he required.

But keeping an ex-lover on his staff? It went against every instinct. No matter that they'd proved they could work together and put those few hours of weakness behind them.

Almost behind them.

Jonas set his jaw and confronted the truth. Not a day passed when he didn't remember in glorious detail the incandescent pleasure of sex with Ravenna. He enjoyed being with her. Her quick wit, her indomitable attitude, her pleasure in so many things he enjoyed, like seeing the gardens come to life, celebrating the completion of each room, even smiling over the antics of Timothy and Hector.

Until a few weeks ago. Something had changed and he couldn't work out what. He only knew he didn't like it.

'Where exactly is it you're going?' Jonas asked as she pleated her skirt with restless fingers.

'Just a few streets away. You can drop me anywhere here. I would have been quite happy catching the train. You really don't need to go out of your way.'

Which was the most she'd said on the whole journey. If he didn't know better he'd think she was babbling.

Ravenna never babbled. She was articulate and composed. Except that day they'd been naked together and ecstasy had stolen her voice. Predictably, arousal stirred at the memory, and a deep-seated satisfaction.

Hell! He shouldn't feel anything like this for Ravenna. Not now, not when he was planning to marry. But the sexual attraction between them hadn't yet dimmed, no matter how hard he tried to ignore it.

Jonas forced himself to concentrate on the traffic rather than the past.

Yet something was wrong and he couldn't ignore it. Over the months at the Hall Ravenna's colour had improved—she wasn't pale and fragile as when they'd met in France. But now that healthy glow had faded.

'Where will I collect you?'

Her head swung round, her eyes large and startled. 'There's no need. I'll catch the train.'

'My business won't take long so I can pick you up whenever you like. Just give me the address.'

'Really, I—'

'Unless you want me to wait now?'

'Up here.' She pointed abruptly at a café. 'If you come by and I'm not here, then just go on without me and I'll find my own way back.'

Jonas suspected she had no intention of meeting him and fobbed him off with a place chosen at random. Once he'd have suspected she was plotting to run away and escape the consequences of her crime but now he knew better. Concern filled him.

'Very well.' He manoeuvred the car into a recently vacated spot and watched her fumble with the door. 'I'll meet you in an hour or so.'

Ravenna nodded and got out, walking away without looking back.

Jonas watched her go, telling himself it wasn't his business she kept secrets. She had a right to a personal life. But the tension in her rigid body was palpable.

He waited till she'd rounded the corner before he got out and followed.

* * *

Ravenna pushed open the clinic door and emerged into the open air. She breathed deep, filling her lungs with the city scents of wet pavement and exhaust fumes. It was better than the not-quite-neutral smell she associated with hospitals and doctors' waiting rooms that dredged up bleak memories.

She grabbed the railing at the top of the few steps to the street and gathered herself, feeling the adrenalin still coursing through her system after the nervous wait to hear the results of those recent tests.

Her hands clamped the metalwork as emotion hit.

'Ravenna?'

She lifted her head to find Jonas on the step below, his face level with hers. She blinked moist eyes and drew in a breath redolent with that tangy scent she always associated with him.

'What are you doing here?'

'Waiting for you.' His voice was harsh and his expression grim. 'Come on.' He took her elbow, his grip surprisingly gentle given his expression. 'Let's get away from this place.'

She followed his gaze to the sign beside the door, proclaiming exactly what branch of medicine the staff practised.

He led her down the street and into the sort of exclusive restaurant in which she hoped one day to work.

She hesitated on the threshold. 'There's no need for this. I'm ready to go now.'

'Well I'm not.' He swept her into the beautifully appointed dining room and secured a quiet table before Ravenna could do more than blink owlishly at the expensive furnishings.

'A drink?' he asked as she seated herself.

'Nothing, thanks.'

'Cognac for me,' Jonas said to the waiter before turning back to her, his eyes steely. 'Don't tell me you wouldn't like something after visiting that place.'

He was right. She *was* on edge and had been all day with that appointment looming. At least it was over. She sank back in her seat with a sigh. 'A sauvignon blanc if you have it, please.' Ravenna smiled at the waiter who nodded and passed over two leather-bound menus before leaving them.

'Are you all right?' Jonas leaned towards her across the fine linen tablecloth, his gaze intent.

'Fine, thanks. Just a little tired.' Yet tension eddied in her stomach. He'd seen where she went, which meant she couldn't fob him off with vague answers. She'd have to explain, which meant revealing what she'd kept hidden all these months.

It would be a relief, she decided. It had been a strain, lying all this time.

She opened her mouth to speak but halted when he leaned across and took her hand in his. It was the first time he'd touched her since—

No. She wouldn't go there.

'Why didn't you tell me you were ill?' His voice was hoarse and Ravenna read intense emotion in his silvery gaze.

'I'm not.' She shook her head, her heart lightening. When she'd left the clinic she'd still been numb, just coming to grips with the news, but now she felt happiness surge. 'I'm healthy.' Her mouth widened in a smile that felt wonderful. She'd been so worried her remission might be short-lived, perhaps because she'd felt so depressed these last weeks.

'Thank God!' His fingers squeezed hers. 'When I saw you go in there…' He shook his head.

'You followed me?'

'You were anxious. I knew something was wrong.'

Ravenna stared. Jonas Deveson had followed her because he *cared* about her? Her heart leapt and she had a struggle to keep calm.

It made no difference that he'd been concerned. There wasn't anything between them. There could never be.

'So it was a false alarm? You thought you had cancer?' He sat back in his seat, still holding her hand. She should pull away, but she liked the sensation and it was probably the last time he'd touch her—he was so adept at keeping his distance now.

Ravenna drew a slow breath. 'No, not a false alarm. I had cancer. I don't now.'

'Ravenna?' Shock lined his face.

'I'm in remission. I have been for a while. This was just another check-up to make sure nothing had changed. I've had several, but this time I thought the results might be—' She shrugged, not wanting to admit she'd been so down lately that she'd half convinced herself her illness had returned.

The waiter arrived with their drinks and, at a signal from Jonas, left without taking their order for food. Jonas reached out and grabbed the glass of cognac, his eyes not leaving hers. He tossed the liquid back in one quick movement then put the empty glass down.

Guilt stirred. Not because she hadn't told him about her illness. That was private. But because he'd obviously been worried.

'I'm sorry, Jonas.'

'Don't be.' His voice was gruff. 'That's excellent news. I'm just…surprised to know you've been ill.' He paused, his fingers threading hers. 'How long has it been?'

Ravenna hesitated. But she was sick of lying. Surely now, when he heard her out, Jonas would give up his idea of revenge against her mother. He'd already had his pound of flesh after all.

She hoped she was right.

'Ravenna?'

'Last year I was diagnosed with leukaemia.' She saw his eyes widen. His firm grip tightened. 'I was advised to have treatment straight away. The cancer was aggressive but potentially curable. And they were right. I'm well now.' Joy made her smile again.

'How long before I met you?'

Ravenna's gaze dropped to her untouched glass of wine then up to the flat line of Jonas' mouth.

'When we met in Paris I'd just come from a Swiss sanatorium. I'd been there, recuperating.'

'I see.' His expression didn't change but his gaze turned laser sharp. 'Why didn't you tell me when we met?'

Ravenna tugged her hand but his grip didn't ease. It kept her anchored within his warm grasp. Could he feel her pulse trip faster?

'It wasn't relevant. It's not the sort of thing to share with strangers.'

'I was hardly that, Ravenna.' His tone made her nape prickle. 'Could it be because you didn't want to admit you needed my money to fund the health resort?'

She sighed. 'You're sharp, aren't you?' Not that it mattered now. He'd have to know it all. She'd just have to do her best to protect her mother.

'Sharp enough to realise if you were recuperating in Switzerland you weren't in my father's Paris apartment, forging his signature.'

Jonas felt his gut plunge hard and fast, like a stone in deep water.

He remembered Ravenna in Paris—proud and defiant, throwing her guilt in his teeth. To deflect him? Of course. And he'd been so wrapped up in his hatred of Piers and Silvia that he hadn't stopped to question.

He'd seen how pale Ravenna was, how delicate her wrist as he shackled it and pulled her to him. He recalled how fragile her body had seemed compared with her in-your-face attitude.

Because she'd been ill.

Too ill to fight back?

Guilt was a raw slash of pain to his belly. He'd bullied her when she was vulnerable. What did that make him?

Jonas dragged his free hand through his hair. No wonder her clothes hadn't fitted. She must have lost weight in therapy. He'd been sure she'd dressed to project waif-like vulnerability for that antiques dealer. He'd been so ready to make snap judgements, hadn't he?

Bile seared his throat as he reviewed that day. He'd stormed in, all violent temper and attitude, and nearly ripped her head off when she'd dared stand up to him.

'Your hair,' he croaked, his windpipe tight. 'That's why your hair was so short.'

Ravenna lifted a hand to the sable curls clustering like a dark halo around her face. 'I'm growing it now.'

'I remember it before. It used to be long.' For months after meeting the teenage Ravenna Jonas had wondered why so many women cut their hair short. There'd been something deliciously appealing about long female tresses.

'Another drink, sir? And something to eat?' He hadn't noticed the waiter approach.

'Another cognac.' He didn't drink much but today he needed it. Confronting the truth had never been so unpalatable. 'Ravenna? Something to eat?'

She looked up and after a moment's hesitation engaged the waiter in a discussion of the day's specials. When she'd ordered he said he'd have the same and finally they were alone.

'It wasn't you who stole my money, was it?' Jonas spoke through gritted teeth. How could he have fallen for her story? Hadn't the evidence pointed to Silvia from the first?

After a lifetime keeping a lid on his feelings, they'd finally erupted with the news of the embezzlement, undercutting his usual clear thinking. Why hadn't he questioned her more closely when she admitted the theft?

Because his blistering anger had needed a target and she was handy. Because she was the daughter of the woman he'd spent years blaming for his father's defection, despite knowing Piers had always sought his own pleasure rather than embracing his responsibilities.

It had been easier taking out his long-simmering fury on Ravenna than dealing with the fact that the person who'd been at the root of so much pain—Piers Deveson—was finally beyond either reproach or reconciliation.

'It was Silvia, wasn't it?'

'Please don't hurt her, Jonas.' Ravenna's hand twisted in his, her fingers grasping with reassuring strength. The shock of seeing her entering that clinic still reverberated through him.

'Jonas?' Solemn eyes of old gold fixed on him. 'I know it was wrong. She had no right to the money. Nor had I.'

'Did you know where it came from?'

'Not till you confronted me in Paris.' Her quick gesture discarded that as a minor issue. But it wasn't. Ravenna had been innocent from the first. She'd claimed responsibility only to protect her mother and then she'd worked like a slave to pay off a debt for which she had no responsibility.

Jonas was torn between admiration for her and deep-seated nausea at what he'd done. He'd used and abused her. He'd taken out his ire on an innocent woman.

'Mamma was desperate. She'd been selling off assets for ages, just to live the way Piers expected. She had no money of her own.' Ravenna shook her head. 'Piers had expensive tastes and in the past he'd bought Mamma extravagant gifts, but he'd never spent money on me. I should have known his generosity to me was out of character.'

'You were sick.' Even now the thought of it smote him a hammer blow to the chest.

'But I should have realised.' Her mouth firmed. 'Maybe I didn't want to think too much about it. Maybe—' His finger to her warm lips stopped her words.

'Stop beating yourself up.' He let his hand drop to the table, noting how she slid her hands into her lap, away from him. Who could blame her after what he'd done? 'You weren't to blame.'

Ravenna leaned forward, the subtle, sweet perfume of her skin enticing. 'You have to understand my mother was desperate. She shouldn't have stolen from you, but she was convinced I needed time and care to recuperate fully. She was terrified I'd have a relapse.'

Jonas nodded, his stomach churning in sympathy with Silvia Ruggiero for the first time. He understood her fear too well. He still felt sick from the shock of believing Ravenna ill.

'Please, Jonas. Please be lenient with her.'

'She should have stayed. Not left you to carry her guilt.' That stuck in his craw.

Ravenna's slim fingers closed over his hand, startling him before sliding away. 'She didn't. She has no idea you'd discovered the loss. I suppose she hoped the money wouldn't be missed or you'd write it off as money to your father.'

'So naïve.' When he started out Jonas had risked every penny to invest then invest again. He never took money for granted, given how he'd worked to acquire it.

'Jonas, what are you going to do to her?' The fear in Ravenna's voice brought him up sharply.

'Nothing.' He watched her exhale on a sigh that left her looking limp. 'Here, drink this.' He lifted her wine glass to her lips, waiting till she held it herself and took a sip.

'Nothing? Really?' She looked dazed. He really *had* been an ogre. And now he felt about two feet tall. 'You won't prosecute?'

'There'll be no gaol, no prosecution. I've had enough of revenge.' Jonas grimaced on the word, its taste souring his tongue. 'How could I prosecute a mother for trying to save her daughter?'

'But I would have been all right without the funds.' It was as if still she didn't believe him—had to test him.

Jonas raised his eyebrows. 'Piers would have looked after you?'

'No. He was unwell by that stage, but no one knew how unwell.' Ravenna's eyes dipped to the pristine cloth. 'I'd have come back to London to work.' She lifted her head. 'I'm a chef. I had a promising position before...' She waved her hand vaguely and Jonas' anger fired. She'd lost her job when she got sick?

'So you were going to return straight to work after cancer treatment, doing long hours in a commercial kitchen?' He knew how gruelling that would be. He'd worked as a waiter in his university years. He'd vowed then to make his living the comfortable way—at a desk rather than on his feet doing split shifts till all hours.

The full brunt of what Ravenna had borne hit him. The illness. The slow convalescence. Dealing with her mother's financial crisis on top of what must be worry about her own finances and career. Then facing down an irate idiot hell-bent on vengeance. How had she coped?

He remembered that first day at the Hall, finding her asleep in the middle of the day and assuming she was lazy. His gut twisted as he realised she must have been exhausted.

'I'm sorry, Ravenna.' The words were too little, too late. 'What I've done to you, what you've been through…I had no right to threaten and take out my anger on you. I should never have forced your hand the way I did.'

'You didn't know.' She smiled wearily. How much she'd borne. The knowledge shafted home his guilt.

'I should have made it my business to know.' Instead of jumping in boots and all.

How could she take it so calmly? He winced, remembering his harsh words and actions. 'I said things I had no right to.' Her pain when he'd accused her of being a gold-digging opportunist like her mother! 'I'm sorry, Ravenna—'

'It's all right.' She looked over his shoulder. 'Here's our lunch.'

The waiter didn't linger but served them swiftly, providing another large cognac for Jonas. He reached for it, wanting that quick burn of fine brandy in his throat, then stopped. His father had always avoided the consequences of his actions and responsibilities. His mother had escaped reality in her own world of gin-fuelled disappointment.

Jonas put the glass aside.

'It's *not* all right, Ravenna.' It was all wrong, in so many ways.

'It is if you're not going to make Silvia pay.' She paused as if waiting for him to confirm it.

'Forget the money. There *is* no debt.' He breathed hard, still grappling with the knot of self-disgust in his belly. 'It was put to good use.'

Her eyes flashed pure gold and Jonas' breathing hitched. 'Thank you, Jonas.'

'Stop being so gracious!'

Her eyebrows arched. 'You'd prefer if I made a scene?'

'You think I'm being melodramatic?' Was any woman so infuriating?

Ravenna smiled and something fizzed in his veins. 'We were both at fault. We both jumped to conclusions and said things we regret. Can't we wipe the slate clean?' Her stomach growled. 'Especially as I'm starving. I was too anxious to eat this morning.'

'Then eat.' He gestured to her plate.

'And we're all sorted?' Her gaze searched his face.

'Absolutely.' What else could he say? She didn't want his apologies. He felt…frustrated.

'Thank you, Jonas. That's very generous. My mother will appreciate it as much as I do when she hears.'

He didn't care what Silva thought. It was Ravenna who concerned him.

'You'll want to leave Deveson Hall.' The thought struck abruptly as she lifted her fork to her mouth.

She took her time chewing. 'You want me to leave straight away?'

'No!' The word shot out with more force than necessary. He didn't want her gone. Not yet. 'I'd like it if you stayed on. Not to work,' he assured her quickly. 'But for the ball. You've worked too hard to get the place ready. It would be a shame to miss it. If you want to stay on.'

Ravenna kept her eyes on her plate. What was she thinking? Tension crawled down Jonas' spine, one vertebra at a time.

He was working on blind instinct. He had no plan in the aftermath of the truths that had rocked his complacent world. He only knew he'd feel bereft if she left now. He needed time to adjust. Time to replace her, his sensible self reasoned.

'Thank you.' Still she didn't look up. It was as if, having his promise that the theft had been written off, she didn't want to connect with him. 'I've never been to a ball and I'd love to see the Hall with the renovations complete. I'll stay till then.'

CHAPTER TWELVE

SHE SHOULD NEVER have agreed to stay. She should have left the same day. But the shock of her sudden freedom hadn't been as welcome as she'd expected.

Ravenna strode up the staircase as if expending energy could erase the dreadful weakness she harboured.

Despite Jonas' assurances that she didn't have to, she'd put long hours into getting the Hall ready. But they'd done nothing to extinguish what she felt for him. If anything her feelings were stronger since his apology and the sight of his horror when he realised she'd been innocent.

Jonas was essentially a decent man despite his plot to make her pay for the stolen funds. And who could blame him for that? His prejudice against Piers and Silvia was understandable, and to have Mamma then steal from him... Ravenna guessed it had been the final straw.

She walked along the corridor, checking all was in order. It was easier to focus on the busy work of housekeeping than think of the future. The ball was tomorrow and then she'd leave. She had no reason to stay.

Except she didn't want to leave Jonas.

Ravenna blinked at an arrangement of roses gracing a hall table. Reaching out to a velvety red petal, she was reminded of Jonas' touch, exquisitely tender as he brushed his fingers over her naked body, his gaze luminous as he'd watched her shiver with delight under his ministrations.

Sharply she sucked in her breath. This couldn't go on.

There was no future for them. She'd gone from being the enemy to a reminder of an episode he'd rather forget. She saw the shadow of guilt in his face whenever he looked at her.

Ravenna pushed open the door to her bedroom then halted as she saw the flat box on the counterpane. Only one person could have left it there.

Her heart seized then leapt to a gallop, gaze riveted on the distinctive embossed name on the box. Every woman in the western world knew that name. It belonged to one of the grandest Parisian couture houses, one whose young chief designer had taken the world of fashion by storm.

Ravenna's hands trembled as she moved closer, lifting the lid to pull back layer after layer of finest tissue.

Her throat closed. The dress was a delicate filigree of bronze shot with blue and amethyst as the light caught it. Ravenna had never seen anything so ravishingly beautiful in her life. She lifted it out—full length, with a wide skirt and tiny, jewelled shoulder straps, it was a modern Cinderella fantasy. Wearing this would make any woman feel special.

Twirling, she hugged it close and surveyed herself in the long glass. The woman staring back didn't look like Ravenna Ruggiero. She was a princess. The belle of the ball.

Except she *was* Ravenna Ruggiero. She'd never be the belle of any ball, especially Jonas Deveson's. Pain tugged her insides and her fingers crushed the sumptuous fabric.

The dress was a generous, extravagant gesture, borne of guilt and shame. Jonas wanted to put the past behind him and tried to make it up to her like this. He thought an expensive dress for his expensive party would make everything okay.

The gift was the embodiment of his guilt. He'd been too gracious to insist she leave immediately. But every time he looked at her in this gown he'd be reminded how he'd treated her.

And she'd remember he thought to buy her forgiveness.

She stiffened, her hands dropping.

That was what rich men did, didn't they? Bought what they wanted? It was what Piers had done with Mamma. Her mother had fallen for Piers hook, line and sinker and in his own way he'd fallen for her. But he'd begun by lavishing outrageously expensive gifts on her, blinding her with his generosity, because that was how the system worked.

Rich men married rich women. They only offered poor women expensive treats in return for—

No! That was not what Jonas was doing. He didn't want her in his bed.

But he did want her silence, her forgiveness, a sense of closure over what had happened between them.

The dress dropped from Ravenna's numb fingers and she turned from the mirror. She wasn't for sale. Just touching the dress brought his earlier accusations about her selling herself rushing back.

She didn't need Jonas' gift. Gorgeous as it was, she'd feel worse for accepting it, as if she'd let herself down. Besides, did she want this stunning gown hanging in her meagre wardrobe? It would be a constant reminder of a time, and feelings, she needed to forget.

Swiftly she scooped up the froth of fabric and tucked it back into its box.

'It's delightful, Jonas. You've done a marvellous job restoring Deveson Hall.' Helena smiled up at him, her china-blue eyes bright with approval and her perfectly sculpted lips curving in an enchanting smile.

He held her close but not too close as they danced. The ballroom glittered as the antique mirrors down one wall reflected the brilliant chandeliers, opulent gowns and lavish jewellery.

Over Helena's shoulder he saw Vivien dancing with a cabinet minister, while the local vet stood in earnest conversation with a sheikh in pristine white robes and a minor royal, no doubt discussing horses, given all three were passionate about them.

Everyone was enjoying themselves. He alone was dogged by a sense of anti-climax.

'Thank you, Helena. I'm glad you approve.' He smiled and pulled her a little closer.

This was the woman he planned to marry. Why couldn't he feel more enthusiasm? The Hall was just as he'd hoped, better, even. Nothing stood in the way of him reaching out and making his dream a reality.

Helena's eyes were as bright as the platinum-set sapphires at her throat. She was interested, expectant. He sensed it with the instinct borne of experience.

'What are your plans, Jonas, now you've completed work on the Hall?' Her voice was warm and appealing. She was intelligent, generous, good company.

And holding her in his arms he might have been waltzing with an aged great-aunt. Where was the spark of attraction he'd once felt?

'Plans?'

She tilted her head to regard him better and he inhaled the subtle designer perfume she favoured. It was like her—elegant, appealing—just right.

Except she wasn't. Not tonight. Something had changed.

'Now you've finished will you move in full time? Commute from here to the city? Perhaps allow the public in for viewings?' Her smile made light of the question, but he read her anticipation.

It was a perfect opportunity to talk of the future, *their* future. Except looking down at her he felt none of the satisfaction he'd felt before.

'I'm not sure yet.' Where those words came from he had no idea. 'But, yes, I'm considering opening the gardens once they're established. I've had heritage and horticultural groups already badgering me about open days.

Apparently my designer has done something quite special with the grounds.'

'They look marvellous already.' Helena took his lead, chatting about landscaping. Only the puzzled expression in her eyes hinted she'd expected something else. Jonas was grateful she was intelligent enough not to press.

For suddenly, on the brink of achieving his long-held goals, he found himself hesitating.

The music ended and they pulled apart. 'Let me get you a drink.' He took her arm and led her through the throng to the end of the room where drinks were being served.

At the vast double doors more people were clustered, mainly men, their dark formal clothes contrasting with the slim form of a woman in a dress of soft, buttery gold.

Jonas stiffened, every sense alert as she nodded and half turned. No wonder half the men in the place where there. Ravenna's smile was enough to stop any man in his tracks.

Jonas' chest tightened, squeezing his heart into a racing beat. The arousal he hadn't felt when embracing Helena surged hard and fast in his groin, betraying the need he hadn't been able to banish.

Ravenna looked good enough to eat. Heat swamped him and suddenly his bespoke tailoring seemed too tight. He wanted to rip his collar undone and shrug out of his jacket.

Then what? Stalk across and haul her to him so her audience knew she wasn't available?

To hell with the crowd, he wanted to hold her for the sheer satisfaction of having her where he wanted her.

The realisation hit in a blinding flash.

She turned again and her skirt belled out. Unlike most of the gowns hers ended at the knees, revealing smooth, shapely calves. She wore no jewellery except glittering earrings, but she didn't need any. She looked graceful and gorgeous with her cap of dark curls and pale gold skin.

Jonas frowned. That dress! What had happened to the one he'd bought? He surged forward.

'Jonas? Is everything all right?'

Helena's voice recalled him to sense. He slammed to a halt and turned, fixing on a stiff smile.

'Of course. I just wanted a word with my housekeeper but it can wait.' Though the effort of holding back almost killed him.

'Is that her? In the brocade? That material is just gorgeous. I've never seen anything like it.'

Unaware of their gaze Ravenna left the group and crossed the room only a few feet away. She was deep in conversation with one of Jonas' business associates, who looked far too suave and smug as he separated her from the crowd.

As they passed the light caught the material of her dress. Jonas blinked, not believing what he saw.

'I believe it's quite unique,' he muttered.

Damn! It *was* unique. It had been woven especially to a design by his artist great-grandmother. Until a couple of weeks ago it had hung in one of the massive state rooms.

Ravenna had rejected his gift—the best Paris fashion had to offer—and instead swanned around his home wearing discarded curtains!

His hands clenched in fists that shook with outrage. So much for his conciliatory gift! Did she deliberately try to provoke? And the way she flaunted herself, monopolising the unattached men!

'I should go and congratulate her,' Helena said. 'She's done a fantastic job here.'

'Later, Helena.' With a mighty effort Jonas unclenched his teeth. 'Let's get you that drink first.'

Ravenna paused in an alcove off the ballroom, catching her breath. It had been months since she'd mixed with more than a handful of people at a time. The London restaurant kitchen with its frantic pace seemed light years ago.

She'd enjoyed herself tonight. When she'd admitted she was the housekeeper many had congratulated her on her work and plied her with questions about the restoration. One or two men had even been a little too attentive, which, while awkward, had done wonders for her bruised ego.

There'd been raised eyebrows among the society women though, and pointed looks at her home-made dress and extra height. Those stares reminded her of childhood peers who'd claimed she'd overstepped the line, presuming to socialise with them.

But Ravenna was no insecure child now. She'd responded with cool courtesy and moved on, refusing to let prejudice spoil the only ball she'd ever attend. Yet the experience re-inforced everything she'd known. Jonas moved in a different world. She was an outsider here and always would be.

Her gaze zeroed in on the couple at the top of the ball-room. He was tall and commanding while she, in figure-hugging midnight satin, was the epitome of cool, English beauty.

Jonas Deveson and Helena Worthington, looking the per-fect couple. Her hand was on his sleeve as she leaned in, wearing a private smile.

A hot knife of jealousy sliced Ravenna's breast. Was that the woman Jonas would marry? The press thought so and guests had speculated about an engagement announcement.

Ravenna couldn't even dislike the woman. She was pleasant and charming, with a down-to-earth friendliness. Ravenna could imagine her here with Jonas and their brood of children. Helena would probably even take to Hector and Timothy.

Ravenna lifted her glass of vintage champagne, trying to wash away the sour tang on her tongue.

What had she expected? That after all that had gone wrong between them, Jonas would feel the same unsettling yearning Ravenna did? That he'd want her over the woman who was patently perfect for him?

She took another sip of the effervescent wine, letting it fizz on her tongue then slide down her aching throat.

Across the room Jonas turned and unexpectedly their

eyes locked. Ravenna's breath stopped as lightning arced through her veins. Her toes curled as if she'd touched a live wire. Her whole body hummed with awareness.

His dark eyebrows came down in a straight line of disapproval.

He couldn't know how she felt. He couldn't! So why was he annoyed? The answer was easy. The sight of her discomfited him. The sooner she left, the better.

Her breath caught on something suspiciously like a sob. She turned abruptly to find herself against a solid chest.

'Ravenna?' It was Adam Renshaw, the horticulturalist. His friendly smile was balm to her tattered soul. 'I've been looking for you. Would you like to dance?'

'Thank you, Adam.' Ravenna was fed up with herself—pining for what she could never have. She had to move on with life. Defiantly she drained her glass and put it down with a sharp click, ignoring the slightly foggy feeling of a little too much champagne. 'I'd love to dance.'

Ravenna switched off the last of the lights and stood in the vast, empty ballroom, revelling in the silence. The ball had been a huge success and she'd enjoyed it, she assured herself, ignoring the pain clutching her chest.

She'd danced for hours and instead of being relegated to the kitchens she'd indulged in champagne and caviar, in a midnight supper on the terrace with Adam and then more dancing. She smoothed her hands down the heavy silk of her skirt, trying to focus on the evening's pleasures rather than the dragging feeling of disappointment that weighted her.

'You've been avoiding me.'

Hand to her throat, she spun towards the door.

A shadow detached from the inky gloom of the wall and blocked her path. Ravenna's heart lurched then thumped against her ribs in a too-familiar needy rhythm.

'You startled me.'

'Did you really expect to keep your distance all night?'

She couldn't read Jonas' expression in the dark but his voice had an edge that cut.

'Why not?' Pride lifted her chin. 'You were busy with your guests. And I didn't need looking after.'

'So I noticed.' He stepped closer, his form growing in bulk as he approached. Even in her heels she felt dwarfed by him, weakened, as if he sucked the energy from the air between them. 'You let Renshaw monopolise you.'

Ravenna stood straighter. 'Adam and I have a lot in common.'

'He'll be moving on to the next job, Ravenna.' Was that a warning in his stern tone? 'He won't stick around.'

'Nor will I.' She'd leave as soon as it was daylight. Seeing Jonas and Helena together had been the impetus she'd needed.

He raised an arm as if to touch her then let it drop. 'You're going together?'

Ravenna frowned, hearing an unfamiliar note in his voice. 'I thought we'd agreed that what I do from here on is my own business, not yours.'

Jonas' breath hissed between his teeth. 'I see.' There was a wealth of disapproval in those two syllables. 'So that's why you didn't wear the dress I gave you.'

'Sorry?'

'If you and Renshaw are an item he'd wonder why you wore clothes bought by another man.'

Jonas' words confirmed her decision not to accept his gift. There was something far too intimate about accepting such a present.

'Adam had nothing to do with my decision. He and I aren't "an item" as you put it.' Pride wouldn't let her hide behind such a deception.

Jonas stalked closer, a hint of his male scent making her nostrils flare.

'You could have fooled me, the way he kept touching you.'

'We were dancing! That's what people do when they

dance.' He was a fine one to talk. She'd seen the way he held Helena. 'I'm going to bed now.'

'Alone?' He moved in front of her as she tried to sidestep and her heart slammed against her ribs. Ravenna sensed tension in him, an aggression that made her neck prickle.

'My movements have nothing to do with you.' Why did that hurt so much, even now? She had to get over this... obsession.

Still he stood unmoving, his bulk blocking her exit.

Ravenna tried to tell herself it was anger stirring butterflies the size of kites in her stomach. 'Instead of giving me the third degree why don't you go to bed? Helena will wonder what's keeping you.' The words shot out on a burst of bravado that left her feeling hollow.

'Helena's gone.'

'Gone? But she was with you, farewelling the guests.' Ravenna had tried not to notice how the blonde beauty had lingered. She'd headed to the kitchens to supervise the packing up so she didn't have to watch the pair.

'Nevertheless, she's gone.' His tone had a ring of finality.

'I should go too.' The air was fraught with tension that sent quivers through her body. Jonas was so close she saw his eyes gleam. If she leaned in they'd touch. She felt his proximity from her tingling lips to her budding nipples and lower, where desire spiralled deep.

His arm snapped out and long fingers circled her bare arm in a bracelet of fire.

'Let me go.' She tried to keep her voice even but it came out in a rush of breathless energy.

'Not till you tell me what's going on. Why aren't you wearing my dress?'

Ravenna tried and failed to tug her arm free. Desperation rose. She needed to get away.

'Because it would mark me as yours, bought as easily as any other commodity.' She shook her head, trying to find her voice in a throat choking closed on a rush of emotion.

'I know you didn't do it because you *want* me. Only because you want to be *rid* of me. But—' she drew a ragged breath and met his eyes '—I am not for sale. You don't need to *buy* me with anything. I told you we were quits. I won't wear your guilt.'

His hand slid up her arm to close on her shoulder. Hard fingers spanned her bare flesh, warming it against the chill inside her.

'You're wrong.' His voice was a low throb, brushing like velvet across her skin and making her shiver. Ravenna squeezed shut her eyes. He only had to speak and she weakened! And his touch…this was impossible.

'Let me go, Jonas.'

For answer he lifted his other hand and cupped her face, his hand engulfing her jaw, imprisoning her so she had no option but to lift her head towards his.

'You're wrong,' he said again and this time she heard a tremor in that deep, rich voice. It mirrored the shiver in his long fingers. 'I do want you, Ravenna. I've never stopped wanting you. Seeing you tonight only confirmed it.'

Stunned, Ravenna stared up at him.

Jonas stared back, committing every detail of her face to memory, his mind supplying the detail the darkness hid. He knew her features as well as his own.

His hand at her shoulder slid down, shaping the supple curve of her back and dragging her in against him.

'That's impossible.'

His bark of laughter was short and humourless. Jonas pulled her closer, higher, cupping her buttocks in an act of flagrant carnality that set his mind spinning. He'd wanted this so long.

'Impossible? Surely this—' he thrust his hips forward, melding them in a move that made his head spin '—proves it.'

Her hands clamped his shoulders. To push him away or

tug him close? He tightened his grip. No way was she waltzing off to her gardener tonight. Not now. Not when her yielding body told him she wanted him too. A sigh escaped her parted lips and it was music in his ears.

Fire coursed through his veins. He burned up with need. Touching her, imprinting her against him stoked the flames.

'Ravenna.' He dipped his head and kissed her neck, triumph filling him as she arched, giving him access to her throat. She tasted sweet as honey, soft and alluring. Impossibly tempting. 'You want me too. I feel it.'

Her hands clutched him. One thigh lifted to slide restlessly along his, inflaming his libido. He shook with the force of standing firm, doing no more than taste.

'No. This isn't right.' But her voice lacked force. It ended on a sigh when he scraped his teeth along the base of her neck and she shivered voluptuously. 'What about Helena?'

'I sent her away.' How could he even think of marrying her when he was consumed by thoughts of Ravenna?

'Away?' Ravenna stirred in his hold and Jonas squeezed his eyes shut, trying to withstand the excruciating delight of her body moving against his.

'It's you I want, Ravenna. All night I've watched you, wishing I was with you. Wishing we were alone so I could do this.' He bent his head and traced the neckline of her dress down to the delicious swell of her breast, fuller now that she wasn't so waiflike. Her gasp of pleasure as he suckled her through the fabric set his blood roaring. He remembered the taste of her naked breast and needed it now.

In one urgent move Jonas backed her against the wall.

'You want me too. Don't you?' Her body responded to his, arching into his touch, but he needed to hear it. 'Ravenna.' His voice shook with the force of holding back. He was on the edge, never so inflamed by desire as now, holding Ravenna's slim form, tasting the musky note of arousal on her skin. 'Tell me.'

'I can't.' Her voice was a thready whisper.

Jonas blinked and lifted his head to look down at the woman he wanted—no, needed. A sliver of moonlight pierced the gloom, revealing confusion on her fine features. But it also showed the slumberous warmth in her eyes.

'Can't or won't?' He let one hand drop to her leg, drawing her dress inch by inch up her thigh, watching her eyes widen then narrow to hooded slits. Her tongue darted out to slick her bottom lip in unconscious invitation.

His groin was tight and hard, needy for her. Only her. He pressed close, imprisoning her against the wall, revelling in the way her thighs parted for him. Yes! She wanted him as much as he did her.

Jonas slid his hand beneath the rucked-up skirt to touch silk stockings then cool flesh. His rough fingers felt clumsy as he circled her inner thigh, drawing another gasp from her.

'Say it, Ravenna.' She drove him crazy! He stroked up to the apex of her thighs, to brush hot silk and feel her quiver. His ears clogged as his blood pounded. His nostrils filled with the scent of arousal. His body grew rigid with the force of holding back.

Fear held him. He didn't trust himself to touch her again. He was too close to losing control.

The brush of her hand against his shirt came out of nowhere, making him start. Her fingers trailed lower and he was stone, set solid with desperate anticipation.

Her voice was a ragged whisper that sounded as if it had been torn from her. 'I shouldn't but I do. I want you, Jonas.'

An instant's shocked stillness then restraint ripped away. Jonas' fingers tangled with hers, fumbling to undo his trousers. The feel of her nimble hands wrenching open his zip almost tipped him over the edge. And when her cool fingers touched his hot flesh…

With a hungry growl he planted his hands at her hips and hiked her up against the wall. Her legs came round his waist in a quick, clumsy movement as between them they hauled her skirt up out of the way. Her breath came in pants that matched his tortured gasps.

Their eyes locked. Jonas never wanted to look away. When Ravenna looked at him like that he could do anything, be anything she wanted.

Unsteadily he reached for her, tracing the lace edge of her underwear, pulling it aside. But he couldn't manage gentle; his hands were too clumsy. He heard tearing and her panties came away in his hand.

Something flared in her eyes. Something that told him she was excited, not afraid. Her legs tightened around him, and suddenly it was too much. He thrust high and hard, burying himself in her heat. She was all around him, hot silk against his erection, long legs circling his waist, hands cupping the back of his neck.

'You're mine.' The words slid through gritted teeth as he thrust again, anchoring her, probing as deep as humanly possible, making her his in the most elemental way.

'Mine,' he growled, feeling tremors begin deep inside her and knowing a fierce, possessive joy that *he* did this to her. He brought her bliss. He saw it in her radiant face, heard it in her hoarse voice, shouting his name, felt it in the pulsing climax that rocked her from the inside out. She came so hard and fast he had no time to think before it took him too, overtaking him with a rush of such force, such violent ecstasy, he doubted he'd survive.

Bracing himself, Jonas rode out a storm of pleasure that wrung every ounce of energy he'd once possessed. It was all he could do to stand. Yet from somewhere he found strength to hold Ravenna. Nothing could have pried her from his possessive grip.

She was his. Nothing in his life had ever felt so right.

CHAPTER THIRTEEN

AFTER ANOTHER URGENT coupling, this time on the newly re-upholstered sofa, Ravenna lay, pulse racing, weighed down by Jonas' solid form. He held her close. His head pillowed on her bare breasts, the dark spill of his hair tickling, and his hand splayed possessively at her hip.

Her heart tumbled in a rush of amazement and pleasure.

Ravenna cradled him as his breathing began to slow, the hot puff of his breath deliciously intimate on her skin.

She couldn't believe what had happened despite the evidence of her own sated body. She could lie here for ever.

But already she saw the sky lighten through the French windows on the far side of the ballroom. Dawn was on its way.

How long had they been here, lost in each other?

Too long. Shocked, she remembered today was the day she left Deveson Hall for good. Left Jonas.

Pain cramped her chest, constricting her breathing.

Jonas stirred. Languidly he licked the underside of her breast, then took her nipple into his mouth, suckling gently. Immediately a fine thread of tension pulled from her breast to her womb, tugging her senses into tingling awareness. Molten heat filled her, turned her boneless all over again.

Her breath caught at the sight of him there at her breast and the thread of pleasure snapped to vibrating tautness.

Yet it was the emotional connection, rather than the physical, that undid her.

How could she bear to walk away?

She had no choice.

The metallic tang of despair filled her mouth. She blinked and looked away, forcing her arms to her sides. They felt empty without him.

'We need to move.' The words rushed out.

'Ravenna?' He lifted his head, silver eyes piercing in the gloom. 'You regret this?'

How could she not?

Yet it was an exquisite memory to hoard for later. Instinctively she knew forgetting Jonas would be impossible.

'This wasn't supposed to happen.' She put her hands on his sturdy shoulders but he didn't budge.

'No. But it was inevitable.'

'Nothing is inevitable.' Except perhaps her weakness for Jonas. The full import of what she felt for him had hit her hours earlier as she'd swayed in Adam Renshaw's arms, trying not to stare at the glamorous couple at the centre of the throng. Trying to tell herself she was mistaken—she could never care for Jonas *that* much. But the hollow in her heart told its own story.

'You're going to marry her.' She saw the shock in his eyes and knew the rumours were true. Pain stabbed.

Again she pushed his unyielding shoulders. 'You need to get off me.' She couldn't bear to look at him now he'd silently confirmed the truth.

'We need to talk.' Still he didn't move.

Ravenna's fingers clawed at his bare flesh, trying to shift him. How could she think when they lay naked together?

'Please, Jonas. Let me up.'

For a moment longer he lay there, then abruptly he was gone.

She'd never touch him again, she realised with a tinge of desperation. Slowly, avoiding his eyes, she sat up, naked but for her suspender belt and silk stockings. Frantically she scanned the floor but couldn't locate her clothes. She couldn't even recall where she'd lost them.

'Here.' Jonas draped something around her shoulders. It was his dinner jacket, she realised as it enveloped her and the scent of his body engulfed her. She wrapped it close, prolonging the moment she had to trust her jelly legs and look for her dress.

Jonas tugged on his dress trousers then turned to her, barefoot and bare-chested. One furtive glance confirmed he looked sexier than ever. And more dangerous, his jaw set stubbornly.

'First up, you're wrong. I'm not marrying Helena.'

Her gaze collided with his, a ripple of shock filling her. 'You're not?'

A frown wrinkled his high brow. 'I'd thought about it.'

Again pain knifed her. 'But you've changed your mind. You've found another bride.'

Slowly he shook his head. 'No. I just realised I couldn't marry her.' His polished pewter stare pinioned her. 'Because of you.'

Elation mixed with disbelief in a potent brew that made her light-headed. Ravenna clutched the lapels of his jacket with stiff fingers.

'I don't understand.' She wanted to hope but something held her back. Maybe the confusion in Jonas' face.

He shoved his hands in his pockets and her gaze dragged down over the bunched muscles in his arms and chest. He'd used that power tonight to pleasure her, taking her with a fervent passion and raw strength that had made her feel positively petite against him. She'd never felt more feminine.

He spread his arms. 'I'd planned to marry Helena. She'd make an excellent wife and mother.' He ticked off points against his fingers. 'We mix in the same spheres. She's intelligent and attractive. Warm-hearted too.'

With each point Ravenna's belly squeezed hard over a

knot of pain. It was one thing to realise she'd been right, but quite another to hear Jonas spell out all the reasons Ravenna would never be right for him.

'I get the picture,' she said before he could continue. 'You want the perfect wife for your perfect life at Deveson Hall.'

'It's not that simple.' He inhaled, his impressive chest rising mightily. Ravenna remembered the feel of it, hot and slick, rough with a smattering of hair that tickled her sensitised breasts.

'No?' She jerked to her feet, unable to sit, listening to his marriage plans. On still-wobbly legs she crossed to one of the French windows, preferring the grey pre-dawn view to Jonas' sharp gaze.

'No.' His voice came from behind her. 'Give me credit for some scruples. How can I marry her when I'm fixated on you? All night my attention kept wandering to you flirting with Adam Renshaw, driving me quietly insane.'

Stunned, Ravenna whirled to find him a few paces away. Big, bold and surly—he was the most intimidating male she'd ever met.

'But you and I aren't…we weren't—'

'Lovers?' His eyebrows drew together. 'Think again, Ravenna.' His look scorched her skin and she pulled his jacket close, as if to hide her wanton eagerness at his possessive stare. He kindled an excitement that turned her bones to water.

'I want you,' he murmured in a voice of rough gravel that abraded her senses. 'I've wanted you from the first and I want you now. I tried to keep my distance, especially when I discovered how wrong I'd been about you. The truth about you only made me want you more.'

He took a step towards her but stopped as she held her palm out.

'That's why I can't marry Helena.' His look was grim. 'Because I want you here, Ravenna, with me. Will you stay?'

His words knocked the breath from her lungs, leaving her

dizzy from shock and lack of oxygen. She put a hand to her thumping heart to stop it catapulting right out of her chest.

He wanted her with him?

He wanted her to replace Helena as his bride?

For a fleeting moment Ravenna pictured herself with Jonas, not just sharing her body, but her life. The picture was so alluring it almost blinded her to reality. For she loved him. She'd fallen for him despite her caution. Fallen for him hard as she learned the sort of man he really was.

Then she remembered what he wanted from life.

She couldn't give him that.

She could never be the woman he needed.

Her knees loosened and she reached out blindly, steadying herself on the window pane, cool from the night air.

Besides, she'd asked if he'd found another bride and he'd said no.

Sheer willpower made her straighten and face him. 'What exactly is it you want from me, Jonas?'

Jonas tried to lock his eyes on her face but they kept straying. Never in his life had he seen a woman so sexy. His jacket hung loose and long on her, but now she'd forgotten to clamp it closed it parted to reveal her satiny skin, a hint of one lush breast and the shadow of her pubis, a dark arrow between her legs. She shifted, inadvertently revealing the suspender strap that secured one of her stockings and his blood thundered in a storm of need.

Twice hadn't been enough. Would he ever have enough of this woman who so intrigued and innocently seduced? From the look on her face she had no idea he fought arousal all over again.

'I want you, here, with me.' The words felt good. *He* felt good, admitting the truth he'd avoided too long. Relief filled him and his mouth tugged up in a smile. He saw emotion flare in her eyes and knew it would be all right. Ravenna wanted him too.

Jonas stepped in, lifting his hand to stroke her cheek. She turned her head and shifted away, making him frown.

'Ravenna?' What was she playing at? 'You feel it too—I know you do. After tonight you can't deny it.'

She swung to face him, her expression guarded. 'In what capacity do you want me, Jonas?'

He shrugged. Lover? Girlfriend? What did words matter?

'As your housekeeper?'

He hesitated. He'd thought about asking her to stay and keep the Hall running as she'd done so admirably, but it didn't seem right.

'Or as your mistress?'

'That's a word I prefer not to use.' It implied payment for services. Ravenna would stay because she wanted to, not because he'd shower her with gifts. He'd been wrong earlier, believing her driven by mercenary motives.

'Or maybe both?' Her husky voice rose half an octave. 'Housekeeper and mistress together? Keeping up the family tradition?'

Jonas shook his head, her words like a smack in the chest. What they shared had been wonderful, incandescent. Why did she twist things?

'I refuse to do to your fiancée what Mamma and Piers did to your mother.' Ravenna planted her hands on her hips, anchoring his jacket wide and inadvertently displaying her nakedness. Jonas' blood pressure soared but he dragged his gaze to her face.

'I'm not Piers.' Her expression remained accusing and he felt anger stir. 'Besides, I told you I have no fiancée. Helena and I have never even discussed marriage.'

Still Ravenna didn't look impressed. What did he have to do to make her admit what was between them? Didn't she realise what a huge decision he'd made, ditching his planned proposal? Had she no inkling of what a momentous concession this was for him, pushing aside his long-held plans? All because of her?

'But you will have a fiancée at some stage, won't you?' Ravenna stepped into his space. She poked an accusing finger into his sternum.

Jonas grabbed her hand, flattening it against his chest. He breathed deep of her sweet cinnamon scent, letting it steady him.

'I want you, Ravenna, and you want me. It's that simple.'

He lifted his free hand to her jaw then let it slide slowly down her throat, between her breasts, to her navel. He felt her skin twitch and she sucked in a huge breath. Pleasure filled him at her responsiveness but he kept his eyes locked with hers. His hand drifted down her belly then slid between her legs to the damp core of her where he'd lost himself so recently. Where he wanted to lose himself again.

Need juddered through him and his body grew rigid. Still she didn't move.

'Remember how good we are together?' His demand emerged gruffly but somehow it sounded more like a plea. Why the defiant look in her eyes? Why hold herself so aloof?

He dragged his hand away but kept her palm planted on his chest.

'I'm not asking you to betray anyone, Ravenna. I'm not talking about some tawdry affair behind another woman's back.' Relief showed on her face and he frowned. 'How could you think that of me? After what my mother suffered from my father's infidelity?'

Ravenna blinked and he thought he read regret in her expression. 'You have your sore spots. Being treated as a mistress, as the other woman, is mine.'

'I'd never ask that of you.'

She shook her head and tried to pull away. He kept her anchored.

'But one day you'll want what you've always wanted, won't you? The dream you've had for years. The perfect wife in the perfect life.' Her eyes were huge and pleading.

'I…' Jonas flattened his mouth. He hadn't thought that

far ahead. 'I just know I can't marry Helena when I need you like this.' He'd never been so honest with a woman in his life. It made him feel raw, almost vulnerable.

'But I'm not the bride for you.' Her voice was cool, devoid of emotion.

Everything in Jonas stilled. He stared into her arresting, haunted face and felt something shift, as if the ground quaked and moved beneath their feet.

He looked at Ravenna and saw something utterly, stunningly new. Why hadn't he seen it before?

'Why not?' His fingers tightened around hers, excitement stirring.

'Oh, Jonas, don't!' Fleeting pain shadowed her eyes before she looked away to their joined hands.

'I'm serious, Ravenna.' He'd been so caught up with the list of wifely attributes he'd compiled that he'd almost ignored one of the essentials: desire for his wife. No, not just desire, he realised as Ravenna's hand trembled against him. Need. A sense of connection.

He'd come to rely on Ravenna in ways that had nothing to do with her work. Being with her completed him—emotionally as well as physically.

His mind raced. Ravenna might not have the social network and impeccable breeding he'd once wanted in a wife, but she had other things: honesty, warmth and loyalty.

With her he felt alive, whole.

'Why not, Ravenna?' The brilliance of it stunned him. 'Don't say you don't want me because I don't believe it. We're good together. We could build a wonderful future.'

She jerked her hand free and spun away, walking with quick, jerky steps to the far side of the window. She wrapped her arms round herself protectively and he frowned. What was wrong with her?

'It wouldn't work.'

'Of course it would.' He started forward but halted, perplexed, at her raised, outstretched hand.

'I'm not the sort of woman you want, remember?' He heard an echo of her old jeering tone. 'I'm not from the right family. I don't move in the right circles. The only reason I know what cutlery to use at a formal dinner is because my mother taught me to clean the silverware!' She hefted a deep breath as if waiting for him to agree.

'I don't care.' It was true. None of that mattered in the face of his need for this warm, lovely woman, who for some unfathomable reason tried to push him away.

'I'm illegitimate. Plus my mother was your father's mistress, for heaven's sake! People would talk.'

'Let them. You're not a woman to let fear of gossip rule your life.' He crossed his arms over his chest. He didn't give a damn what others thought, except for Ravenna's sake, knowing how comparisons with Silvia and Piers could hurt her. He'd just have to protect her from that.

She shook her head and he saw desperation in her face as she moved into the dawn light. He wanted to cuddle her close and make her forget her doubts, but he respected her too much to dismiss her concerns. After all, he'd been the one who wanted a wife who was aristocratic and socially assured.

'Ravenna, none of that matters any more, truly. Not now I've found you.' Why couldn't she understand?

'It will one day. You'll wake up and wonder why you settled for me. Don't you see?' She flung her arm wide in a slashing gesture. 'I've never worn jewels or haute couture in my life and wouldn't know how to start. Listen,' she added when he made to close the gap between them. 'I grew up poor. It's what I know, what I'm used to. All this—' another wide gesture '—isn't me. As a little girl my favourite dressing gown was one my mamma made from a bedspread her employer was going to throw out. I wore handmade clothes and made do with second-hand everything.'

'Which made you resourceful.' Why did she think that counted against her? 'Those silk curtains never looked so good before you wore them.' He grinned, remembering how the fabric had moulded her slim, ultra-sexy body.

'You're not listening!' She stomped her heel, making him smile. He loved her passion.

'I'm listening, sweetheart. But I don't hear anything important.' He stepped closer. 'Nothing you've said makes me stop wanting you. We can build our future together. We'll be happy, I know it. You love the Hall and so will our kids.'

Excitement sizzled in his blood as he imagined it. But a chill scudded through him as she met his eyes. She looked... defeated. In all the time he'd known her, despite everything he'd thrown at her, he'd never seen her look so bleak. She stretched out her arm to ward him off, her hand cool against his skin.

'Ravenna?' Now she worried him.

'It wouldn't work.' Ravenna swallowed hard and her fingers trembled against his chest. 'You want to make Deveson Hall into the home you never had.'

Jonas nodded, bewildered.

'You want it to be a real family home, with your children to carry the Deveson blood and traditions into another generation.' Ravenna's hand fell. Where her palm had been the dawn chill brushed his skin like a premonition of disaster.

'You'd have to give all that up if you married me. I can't be the wife you want. Ever.' She drew a sharp breath and fear drilled deep inside him. 'I can't give you those children, Jonas. Not children of your blood. The cancer treatment left me infertile.'

Her mouth twisted in a pained smile as she took in his silent shock. Then she turned and left the room, leaving him dazed and gutted.

CHAPTER FOURTEEN

Ravenna walked slowly along the meandering street, grateful of the shade cast by the tall houses. With her basket full of market produce she should be planning the lunch she'd cook. Mamma would need it after starting her cleaning job well before dawn and Ravenna needed sustenance before her long shift at the café.

She'd make something special, something intricate enough to stop her thoughts straying to England and Jonas.

Naturally it didn't work. It hadn't worked all week, since she'd arrived to visit her mother, now living in a tiny apartment in this large, anonymous Italian city.

She juggled the basket more securely on her arm, inhaling the scent of basil. Instantly an image sideswiped her—of Jonas tasting her home-made pesto. Of the way pleasure crinkled the corners of his eyes and his rare smile made her stomach somersault.

Ravenna blinked, hating the scratchy heat blinding her vision. She'd done the right thing, leaving that morning. What else could she have done? Stayed on as Jonas' mistress till he was ready to move on to a woman who could give him all he wanted? She'd already broken her heart, falling for a man who she couldn't have. Having an affair with him would have shattered it to irreparable smithereens.

The stark horror on his face when she'd admitted she was barren was something she carried with her every moment.

Her mouth flattened. Had she really hoped she'd reveal the truth and he wouldn't care? Not Jonas. Not the man who'd made it his mission to fill the void in his life with what he'd always dreamed of: a family of his own.

Ravenna knew about his past and guessed at his parents' neglect. She'd heard the tension in his voice as he made light of loneliness and isolation. She'd felt the tremor of guilt rack his body for tragedy he'd been unable to prevent. She'd seen his passion for the estate that was more family to him than his parents had ever been. She *understood* his need to belong there and create what he'd never had.

Ravenna tried to take solace from the fact that he'd *cared* about her. Enough to want marriage.

But that made it all worse. Better if they'd never grown close, never shared—

She shook her head. She couldn't bring herself to wish that. Even now she couldn't regret loving him.

Every limb was heavy as she turned into the old apartment building and dragged herself up the stairs. Crossing the tiny landing at the top, she took a deep breath and worked to twist her mouth into a semblance of a smile.

'I'm back.' She pushed open the door and stepped inside. 'I stopped at your favourite *pasticciera* for a treat.' Money was tight but—

'Ravenna.' The deep voice curled around her, spiralling deep to fill the aching emptiness inside. She froze as the wound in her heart that she'd tried unsuccessfully to cauterise reopened.

He was here, filling the tiny hall.

Searing grey eyes fractured her shell of composure. His dark hair had a rumpled look as if he'd tugged his hands through it. In jeans and a casual, open-necked shirt he looked devastatingly attractive and potently male.

'Jonas!' Was that her voice, that yearning gasp?

'Here, let me.' He dived to rescue the wicker basket that dangled from her nerveless fingers.

The brush of his hand on hers sent her blood racing and brought her numbed brain back to life.

Ravenna snapped her mouth shut, her brain fumbling to take in the fact he was here, not a figment of her needy imagination. 'Where's my mother?'

'She's gone out for a while. Don't worry, she's fine. She just thought to give us time alone.'

Why? What had he said to convince her mother to leave? Questions burned in Ravenna's brain but she couldn't wrap her tongue around the words. Everything was an effort. Her chest ached and she realised belatedly she'd forgotten to breathe.

'Why are you here, Jonas?'

'Shall we?' He gestured to the cramped living room.

Instinctively Ravenna shook her head. 'I can't do this, Jonas. I don't want to talk.'

Something flared in his eyes, turning them the colour of a summer storm. 'Neither do I.' Tingling spread out from her feminine core at the look on his face. 'But we need to. Please, Ravenna.'

How could she walk away? She'd done it once. She didn't have the fortitude to do it again. But did she have the self-control to face him?

'In the kitchen.' If she kept herself occupied maybe she'd be able to hear him out without revealing her feelings.

Her legs trembled as she led the way into the tiny alcove that passed for a kitchen. It shrank to minuscule as his wide shoulders filled the doorway and her heart faltered. This close she smelled his citrus and warm male scent and a pang of longing shafted through her.

'Ravenna?'

She avoided his searching look and lifted the basket from him before scooting back to the corner bench. She busied herself unloading fresh food.

'Why are you here, Jonas?'

'Won't you even look at me?' Her pulse pattered faster and she turned to wash her hands.

'Just say what you have to say, Jonas.'

'I'm sorry.'

She faltered as she flattened garlic with a knife.

'You have nothing to apologise for,' she said finally, her voice scratchy. 'You were honest. That's all I could ask.'

Her hands moved with the ease of long practice as she assembled the rest of the ingredients, peeling and chopping an onion with barely a fumble. Thank goodness for routine! She could pretend to focus on that rather than the man just a few paces away.

She wanted to cup his strained face in her palms and nuzzle that strong neck, feel again the heat of his embrace.

Ravenna blinked. Better if she could thrust him out of the door. But nothing would shift him until he was ready. She remembered his formidable power, how he'd held her weight easily that last night as he took them both to ecstasy. Heat razed her last crumbling defences and she dropped the knife on the bench with a clatter.

'I can't do this.' Her voice wobbled. 'Can you go now?' She couldn't look up, instead bracing herself on the bench so she wouldn't slump to the floor.

'No.' The word came from so close it furred the nape of her neck. 'I won't leave.'

'What?' Her head swung up. His face was so close she could count the tiny lines raying out from his eyes.

'I love you, Ravenna. I'm not leaving.'

She pressed the heel of her hand to her chest, trying to draw in enough air to stop the spots wheeling in her vision.

'You…?'

'I love you.' His eyes shimmered and she felt the warm caress of his breath on her upturned face. '*Ti amo,* Ravenna.'

'That's not possible. You didn't—'

He brushed a curl back behind her ear and her heart contracted at the tender gesture. Heat traced down her throat then dived, arrowing straight to her heart.

'I didn't say it earlier because I didn't realise.'

Ravenna shook her head, unable to summon the words to contradict him. It wasn't love he felt.

'I know that makes me a stupid, slow-witted fool.' His wry half-smile made her unwilling heart flip. 'But you see, sweetheart, I've never been in love before. I don't have any experience to draw on.' His voice hit a deep register, trawling along her bones and insinuating its way into her soul.

Trying not to hear the tension in his voice, she shook her head. 'It's not love. It's lust.'

'Is that all it was for you?'

'No, I—' She swallowed hard, watching lightning sheet across those fathomless eyes. 'You're feeling regret, that's all. You feel sorry for me.'

'Sorry? I'd like to wring your neck for walking out on me like that.' But there was no fire in his words, just pain. 'Do you know how worried I've been? Anything could have happened to you.'

Dumbfounded she stared into his hard-chiselled face. 'I can look after myself.'

His eyes bored into hers and the world quaked.

'I know,' he said at last. 'That's what I'm afraid of. That you don't need me the way I need you.'

'Jonas?' Finally she let herself register what she'd been trying to avoid—the pain drawing his features tight. Without planning it she fitted her palm against his jaw. He clamped it to the roughened silk of his skin, and she shivered as a blast of pleasure hit her at the contact.

'Do you know how I've tortured myself thinking I'd never persuade you to come back? I'm a wreck.'

He didn't look a wreck. He looked more decadently delicious than any pastry she'd ever concocted.

'I love you.' Touching his face, she felt his mouth shape the words, making them real. 'I lust after you, Ravenna, that's a given. But I love you too. I've loved you for weeks, months, I think, but I didn't realise till the ball.'

Her heart pounded on her ribs and she swayed, mesmerised by what she saw in Jonas' eyes. Could it be true?

'And I think you love me too.' His voice was raw with tension.

'Of course I do.' That was the worst of it.

Jonas gathered her close in possessive arms and Ravenna wanted to cry out at the poignant pleasure of it. 'But that doesn't change anything.' She braced herself against his hard chest as he leant in. 'Jonas! Please!'

He nuzzled her neck and Ravenna's world slid out of focus.

'Jonas, you need to listen.'

'I'm listening,' he murmured against her ear, then bit her lobe, sending pleasure streaking through her. 'And it changes everything. The way you invented objections back in England, I couldn't be sure you really cared.'

'I care.' The words slipped out unbidden. She cradled his head as he trailed fiery kisses down her throat and she arched back against his arm, letting herself steal one more desperate moment in his embrace. 'I tried not to but I couldn't help myself.'

'Even after I'd been such a bastard.' It wasn't a question. He held her so tight their heartbeats melded.

The wonder of it, having him here, having him say he loved her, was too much. Her emotions were all over the place. Hot tears leaked down her cheeks. Through the months of tests and treatment she hadn't cried but now—

'Don't cry, my love.' Jonas brushed them away with unsteady hands. 'I'll make it up to you, I swear it.'

'You can't.' She tried to tug out of his embrace but he wouldn't let her. 'Please, I can't think when you hold me.'

Jonas traced his thumb over her bottom lip. 'I'll remember that next time I want to win an argument.'

'There won't be any arguments. We—'

'Of course there will be. You're a passionate, headstrong woman.' His tone turned the words into a compliment. 'And I'm used to getting my own way. So forget right now about telling me we won't stay together. I died a thousand deaths not knowing where you were.' He threaded his fingers through her hair, holding her so she had no choice but to meet his eyes. 'It took far too long to locate you. I'm not letting you go.'

'You're forgetting one thing.' It was the hardest thing she'd ever faced, looking into Jonas' fiercely tender expression and knowing she had to pull back.

'If you're talking about children, stop right there. If it's a choice between children and you, there's no contest. It's you I want.'

For one perfect moment Ravenna stared into his face and knew he genuinely believed that. Wonder filled her, a joy that turned the dingy little kitchen into a grand, sunlit chamber, its pock-marked ceiling into a Tiepolo masterpiece.

She hugged that incandescent moment to herself a little longer then swallowed hard.

'I know you believe that, Jonas. And I love you for it.'

His embrace tightened and she'd never felt safer or more treasured. Finally she moved to pry his hands loose.

'But I can't do that to you. I know how important family is to you.' It was the dream that had sustained him since childhood. 'One day you'll regret tying yourself to me and I can't bear to watch that happen.'

'*You* are my family, Ravenna. You're all I need. How could I give you up?'

She shook her head. 'I won't strip you of your dreams, Jonas.'

His darkening gaze meshed with hers and she felt she looked right into his heart.

'They were dreams, Ravenna, concocted by a needy kid. I'm a man now and I know what I want, what I need. I need *you*. Always. For ever.' He swallowed hard and her heart went out to him. She felt the same way.

'As for kids, we can adopt, or grow old together without them, you, me and a gaggle of dogs and horses.' He shook his head. 'How many people have the chance to be with the one they love, Ravenna? Don't throw what we have away. Don't ask me to. I can't do it.'

For the first time Ravenna dared admit a sliver of hope.

'It's a gaggle of geese, not dogs,' she whispered when she found her voice.

His smile snatched her breath. 'We can have those too. Anything you want.' His smile faltered. 'Just don't send me away.'

'I can't, Jonas. I can't let you do this.' She felt stretched thin by the effort to keep strong.

'You want to see me as a lonely recluse, is that it?'

'You wouldn't be lonely long.' A knife pierced her at the thought of Helena offering Jonas comfort.

'I suppose you're right.' He gave an exaggerated sigh. 'Not with Silvia living in Deveson Hall's Dower House.'

'The Dower House? That's impossible. You hate her!'

'But if I offer her a home you'll visit her, won't you?' He nodded. 'Yes, I'm that desperate, Ravenna. Besides, she brought you up to be the woman you are, so presumably there's more to her than I thought.' He drew a deep breath. 'It may take me a while but I thought I should try to start again with her, if I can do it without the past tripping me up.'

Ravenna shook her head, pride in him stirring. Jonas truly was remarkable. He'd do that for her?

'I can't believe she agreed.'

'She'd do anything to see you happy, love. That made us unexpected allies.'

The idea boggled Ravenna's mind. 'She thought this would mend things between us?'

'It's a start, isn't it?' His eyes searched hers, his expression serious. 'None of us can know the future, Ravenna, but

I know this—I wouldn't be complete without you. I want you as my wife.' He stopped her protest with a finger to her lips. 'You can work as a chef instead of being chatelaine of the Hall. You can shock the county by wearing soft furnishings instead of buying clothes. You can do whatever you like so long as you promise to stay with me.' He hefted in a huge breath. 'I love you, Ravenna Ruggiero. My life could never be complete without you.'

Her heart was bursting. Ravenna swiped her cheek with the heel of her hand. 'That's not fair,' she gulped through a knot of emotion. 'How can I say no to that?'

His blinding smile cracked the last of her defences.

'Say yes. Say you'll marry me.'

'I'll agree to live with you.' Despite the flood of happiness, caution weighed. One day he'd realise what he gave up in taking a barren wife.

'Agreed. Live with me now and in a month we'll marry.'

Despite her battered feelings, Ravenna choked back a smile. 'Don't be impossible.' Jonas leaned in and kissed her throat, her jaw, working his way to her mouth until she gave in. 'Make it five years.' Had she really said that?

'Two months,' he shot back, his eyes gleaming.

'Four years.' Surely by then he'd realise his mistake and she would have a store of memories to sustain her.

'Three months.' Jonas slid his hand down her side, brushing the side of her breast, then letting it rest on the swell of her hip.

Ravenna's breathing hitched and her brain spun dizzily. 'Three years.'

'Oh, love, you drive a hard bargain.' He leaned in, eyes glittering, and kissed her softly on the lips.

Ravenna couldn't resist Jonas at the best of times. When he told her he loved her with every second breath she didn't have the will power to withstand him. Happiness had crept up on her and now it filled her with a blaze of optimism that finally overcame gnawing doubt.

She took his proud, patrician face in her trembling hands and kissed him back with all the urgent passion and deep, abiding love she could no longer deny.

'Don't look so worried, love,' Jonas said later as she sat, cuddled close on his lap. 'We have each other. That's all that matters. And as for the rest—' he shrugged '—we'll take each day as it comes.'

He paused, his lips twitching. 'Now about those three years. I have a counter offer...'

EPILOGUE

Ravenna sat in the shade of a chestnut tree and watched Jonas, blindfolded, tumble to the ground, pulled by eager young hands. Chiara and Josh giggled as their dad groaned theatrically then reached to tickle them. There were screams as they and Vivien's son, Ben, tried to elude him but the five-year-olds were no match for Jonas' long reach.

Gleeful squeals of 'Mamma! Help!' filled the glade and with a grin Ravenna moved to get up.

'No, don't move.' Her mother was already on her feet. 'You look so comfortable. Stay.'

Ravenna subsided, content to bask in the pleasure of watching her family. She'd held out against Jonas as long as she could, eventually agreeing to marry him a year to the day after he'd arrived at the apartment in Italy. He'd used every wile to persuade her and she'd loved every minute of his loving persuasion.

He'd even followed through with his offer of a home for her mother. To their credit Mamma and Jonas were doing their best to put the past behind them and just recently her mother had moved into the Dower House permanently instead of using it as a base for short-term visits.

Jonas had mellowed too, as if the love they shared gave him the strength to accept the complexities of his parents' failed relationship and admit the possibility Piers and Mamma had, whatever their faults, genuinely cared for each other.

Every day with Jonas was a blessing. And the blessings had continued when they adopted the twins three years ago. Jonas had insisted they needn't adopt, that she was all he needed. But the love they shared was so deep and strong it seemed natural to share it further. Each day they learned together, finding parenting a challenge and a reward.

'No, Toby!' Jonas collapsed with a huff of laughter as their Basset Hound, a recent rescue dog, launched himself at them, massive ears flopping and tongue licking.

The children squealed with delight, waking a cross-breed pup that had been asleep at Ravenna's feet. With a yelp of excitement it bounded over to join the melee.

'You might have come to save me.'

Jonas stood, smiling down at her. As ever, her heart gave a skip of pleasure as she met his warm gaze. She'd been a fool ever to doubt his love.

'Sit with me?' She patted the blanket beside her.

'I thought you'd never ask.' He looked over his shoulder. 'If you think Silvia can cope?'

'Of course she can. She revels in it.'

Jonas settled himself and warmth seeped through her as he wrapped his arm around her. 'Happy, love?'

'Always.' Ravenna sank into his embrace. She glowed with excitement. She'd been cautious so long, scared to hope, but the doctor had assured her everything was normal. The miracle she'd never looked for had happened.

'Jonas, I've got something to tell you.'

'Something good?'

'Absolutely.' She lost herself in his smile. 'There's a date we need to mark on the calendar.' Her hand slipped protectively to her abdomen and his gaze followed the movement.

A muffled shout drew the twins' attention but when they looked it was to see Mamma and Daddy cuddling. They did that all the time, so Josh and Chiara turned back to the pups.

It was Silvia who watched Jonas stand and gather his wife

up in his arms as if she was the most precious thing in the world. He hugged Ravenna close and her trill of laughter floated on the warm air.

Silvia smiled. Jonas Deveson was the best thing ever to happen to her darling Ravenna.

Life was very, very good.

* * * * *

COMING NEXT MONTH FROM
HARLEQUIN *Presents*

Available October 22, 2013

#3185 MILLION DOLLAR CHRISTMAS PROPOSAL
by Lucy Monroe

Vincenzo Tomasi needs a nanny for his niece and nephew by Christmas, and the million-dollar salary on offer is more tempting than anything in Santa's sack! Will innocent Audrey risk everything in the most unlikely interview process ever?

#3186 A SCANDAL IN THE HEADLINES
Sicily's Corretti Dynasty
by Caitlin Crews

Newly single Alessandro Corretti escapes the press and sets sail on his yacht...only to be confronted by the woman who destroyed his heart months before. But at sea there are no rules, and Alessandro will take what he wants.

#3187 THE CONSEQUENCES OF THAT NIGHT
At His Service
by Jennie Lucas

When one night with his housekeeper, Emma, has serious repercussions, Cesare must break his own vow—and say *I do* for the sake of his heir. Now he'll expect his new bride to be *sharing* his bed, instead of making it!

#3188 NEVER GAMBLE WITH A CAFFARELLI
Those Scandalous Caffarellis
by Melanie Milburne

To reclaim her birthright Angelique Marchand tracks down her sworn enemy, Remy Caffarelli, to the Middle East. But when she's found in his hotel room, they're forced to marry! Now Remy wants to exploit their marriage for business...*and* pleasure.

HPCNM1013RA

#3189 A DANGEROUS SOLACE
by Lucy Ellis
Gianluca Benedetti might not initially recognize Ava Lord, but the memories soon come rushing back! Exploring their reignited passion, Ava realizes the danger of opening her heart, as the closer he gets, the more cracks in her armor appear....

#3190 SECRETS OF A POWERFUL MAN
The Bond of Brothers
by Chantelle Shaw
Salvatore Castallano is haunted by the accident that left a blank in his memory. His young daughter is the one bright light in his dark existence. He'll do anything for her...even move Darcey Rivers—a delicious temptation—into his castle!

#3191 VISCONTI'S FORGOTTEN HEIR
by Elizabeth Power
Magenta is finally on track after suffering from amnesia. But, meeting Andreas Visconti's familiar gaze, she *knows* he's the father of her child! It's crucial she decipher the scattered puzzle of her mind and recall more than just memories of his touch....

#3192 A TOUCH OF TEMPTATION
The Sensational Stanton Sisters
by Tara Pammi
CEO Kimberly Stanton has rocked the international business world with the announcement of her marriage to outrageous Brazilian bad-boy tycoon Diego Pereira, *and* a pregnancy! If salacious rumors are already spreading, who can say what lies ahead for society's most notorious couple?
